The Dewstone Quest

D0928491

Elizabeth Pewsey was born in Chile to a South American mother and an English father – her Argentinian grandmother was a poet and, she says, 'as nutty as a fruitcake'! Both parents were writers and great travellers, and she lived in India as a child before the family came back to England, where she finished her schooling and went to Oxford University. She now lives in Somerset with her husband and two children.

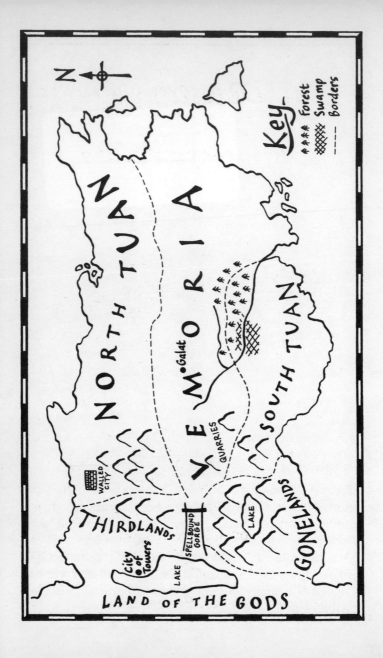

The Dewstone Quest

ELIZABETH PEWSEY

Orion Children's Books
and
Dolphin Paperbacks

The first book in the trilogy

The Talking Head

First published in Great Britain in 1997
as an Orion hardback
and a Dolphin paperback
by Orion Children's Books
a division of the Orion Publishing Group Ltd
Orion House
5 Upper St Martin's Lane
London WC2H 9EA

A catalogue record for this book is available
from the British Library

Typeset by Deltatype Ltd, Birkenhead, Merseyside.
Printed in Great Britain by Clays Ltd, St Ives plc

ISBN 1 85881 303 4 (hb)
ISBN 1 85881 304 2 (pb)

Remembering
Umbriel
the original Dollop

Signs, Dreams
and Portents

Signs, dreams and portents in this world and in the Otherworld which told of the coming of the Red One who would claim the Dewstone and stir up no end of trouble for the future of Vemoria, Tuan and the Land of the Gods.

That night, Hal dreamed he was in America. Visiting his cousin's cousin, and finding himself in a wasteland of snow with Erica's evil laugh ringing in his ears. Then he was in an orchard, full of apples, and then the apples were no longer on the trees, but laid out on a table. In a nightmare way, he knew there was danger for a lost boy, a boy with red hair. Ben, from school. How odd, thought Hal, that he should be in America, too.

Then he saw the canals, and knew he wasn't in America at all, but in Vemoria.

'Look,' said Jouri as he stabled his donkey. 'What a sunset, eh?' His eyes narrowed as he saw the shapes outlined against the blood-red setting sun. 'Dragons,' he said. 'At sunset. Something's up.'

The Numens looked at the tree outside their barn and watched the leaves turn one-by-one to a flaming red. The tree blazed for a few brilliant moments, and then was bare against the snow.

Snowballs fell on the borders of the Gonelands, the size of double handfuls of snow. 'The size of Dewstones,' parents told their children.

On the cliffs of the mountains by the chasm people saw strange writing, runes, which stood out clearly from the shadows, and then vanished.

Ben slept deeply and peacefully. He dreamt that he found a stone, and his father had come back home again, and it was as though he had never been away. Then the voice of his aunt drifted into his dream, telling him to get up, he was going to be late for school, and the dream was gone.

It was a good dream, I'm sure of it, Ben said to himself as he pulled on his shirt. Pity I can't remember anything about it.

In the Walled City, the soothsayers looked up into the sky and then into their own minds. 'The Dewstone,' said one Tuan to another. 'The red-haired boy is coming for the Dewstone.'

One

'I HATE FOG.' GILLY SHIVERED AND PUSHED HER hands into her pockets.

'It's very thick,' said Hal, pulling up his jacket collar.

'Snow,' said Ben in a surprised voice as he disappeared.

'Always has to be different, Ben,' grumbled Hal.

'Ben!' shouted Gilly. 'Ben, where are you?'

Silence.

The fog was becoming thicker and thicker. 'Ben!' yelled Hal. 'Don't play games, if you don't call out, we can't find you.'

'Ben, Ben!'

The words were muffled by the fog, which was swirling around them and getting into their eyes and mouths.

'He could be in the road; if a car comes, they won't see him.'

'Anybody in a car will have stopped by now,' said Gilly. 'Either that or driven into the nearest lamp-post.'

'I don't see what we can do,' said Hal. 'If he won't answer …'

'I don't think he can hear us,' said Gilly. 'Do you think we can find our way home?'

'It isn't far,' said Hal. 'We need to follow the kerb, then we should be okay.'

Thunk.

'Hal? Hal, are you all right?'

'That was the letter box,' said Hal.

'Then our gate must be here on the right.'

'Pity about my nose and teeth,' said Hal. 'It's nice to have sympathy.'

They groped their way to their front door and fell into the hall. 'Mum,' shouted Gilly. 'We're back, but we've lost Ben.'

Mum was sitting in the dining room, her computer set up on the dining room table, books and papers strewn around it. She worked as a translator, and had a big job on at the moment.

'Ben?' she said, getting up from the table. 'Lost? How?'

'In the fog. Just now, when we were walking back from school.'

'Surely it isn't thick enough ...'

Mum opened the back door and peered out. Wafts of cold foggy air billowed into the kitchen. 'Oh dear,' she said, shutting the door. 'I see what you mean. Wasn't Ben with you?'

'He was, until he wasn't,' said Gilly.

'It's his own fault,' said Hal. 'He's hopeless, that boy.'

'He is not,' said Mum firmly. 'Don't you start on about him, hasn't he had enough of that at school?'

'Okay, okay. He's not too bad a kid, really, except that he's got a head full of maggots.'

'Maggots?' said Gilly. 'That's a disgusting thing to say.'

'It's not,' said Hal loftily. 'Maggots in the head means you've got a lot of wild ideas. It's a very old expression, I read it in a book. And liked it.'

'You would.'

'We'll have to find him,' said Mum.

'How? You can't see an inch in front of your nose,

we've called and called, and he doesn't answer; what else can we do?'

'You don't think those others have been lying in wait for him, do you?'

'What, the bullies of 9K?' said Hal scornfully. 'Not them.'

Hal had grown a lot recently, and the boys who'd been having a go at Ben earlier in the term were a weedy lot. 'Ben's been okay since he's being walking with us, they wouldn't mess with him again, not after all that fuss.'

'It's Ben's fault if they have,' said Gilly. 'He's so wet, and he's small, and those silly specs he wears ... no, Mum, don't put on your moral face. I quite like Ben, but he doesn't help himself at all, honestly he doesn't.'

Mum's mind had turned to other things. 'This fog is very thick,' she said, looking out of the window. 'And it seems ... well, restless.'

'Restless?'

'I know what Mum means,' said Gilly. 'Moving about a lot, which fog generally doesn't. And why did it come whooshing into the kitchen when Mum opened the back door? You'd expect the warm air to go out, wouldn't you?'

'Maybe,' said Hal.

'It's been a day of surprises,' said Mum. 'Do you know, there's an apple tree in the garden coming out in blossom? In November!'

Hal and Gilly stared at her, transfixed.

'We haven't got an apple tree in the garden,' Gilly said at last. 'Only a pear and plum. The old apple tree fell down two years ago.'

'I know that; this one must have seeded itself and grown without our noticing it. It's quite a size, too.' Her mind went back to Ben. 'I'd better take a torch and go along the road.'

'He may have got home,' said Gilly. 'Why don't you ring his aunt?'

'I will,' said Mum, and went to the phone.

No reply.

'Try Mrs Hibson,' suggested Gilly.

'Mrs Hibson?'

'She lives across the road from Ben. When his aunt's out, and if she's forgotten to leave any tea for Ben, he goes across to Mrs Hibson.'

Mum was shocked. 'Do you mean Ben often goes home to an empty house?'

'Course,' said Gilly.

'You should ask him here for tea.'

'No, mother dear, you can't get at us for that,' said Gilly. 'We've tried, although I'm not sure I want him here for tea, looking at us with those anxious brown eyes, gives me the creeps.'

'Gilly!'

'Sorry, Mum.'

Mum was dialling. 'Mrs Hibson? I'm sorry to bother you, but I wondered if Ben was with you. He was walking home from school with my two, when they got separated in the fog … What fog? Have you been out? You have, and there's no fog where you are? That's very strange, it's as thick as can be here. No, we'll look for Ben, of course we will, don't worry.'

'No fog there?' said Hal.

Mum shook her head. 'Isn't it odd? I think I'd better take the torch and go and have a look for Ben.'

'We'll come,' said Gilly.

'No,' said Hal. 'I mean, he might turn up here.'

'That's true,' said Mum, pulling on her jacket. 'Have

something to eat, I won't be cooking for a while yet; I've got to do some more work.'

'Why didn't you want us to go with Mum?' cried Gilly, as the door closed behind their mother. 'She mightn't be safe out there.'

'Mum's quite able to look after herself,' said Hal. 'Come on, we're going out to have a look at this apple tree. Where's my torch?'

Gilly discovered it at the bottom of the fruit bowl. 'It's very feeble,' she said, giving it a shake.

'Needs new batteries,' said Hal.

'Quick, then,' said Gilly. 'Before Mum gets back with Ben.'

'I bet she won't find Ben.'

'Why not?'

'Remember the mist?'

'What mist? Oh, no, Hal. It couldn't be. Not again.'

Gilly's mind flew back to the summer, when she and Hal had visited a museum in the nearby castle and had walked into a mist and out into another world.

'That was a different kind of mist,' she said. 'It was a light mist, not fog like this. Besides, we're still here. And there aren't any burial slabs for us to be whisked away through.'

Hal was remembering, too. It had been a shock when they had passed through into another, parallel world, and found themselves caught up in the struggles of two warring countries. 'Wonder how the talking head is,' he said, as they peered through the tangle of brambles at the bottom of the garden.

'And his raven,' said Gilly. 'Still nagging away, I expect.'

'Maybe the raven's bending Ben's ear right now.'

'I don't believe it, Hal. Why should Ben slip through into Tuan or Vemoria?'

'Why did we? It just seems very suspicious, this funny fog which is only around here, and then there's this apple tree. And besides, there was that dream I had.'

'At least there's no sign of Erica,' said Gilly.

They looked silently up at the tree which was just visible in the thin beam of Hal's fading torch.

'It's not only blossom,' said Gilly at last.

'No,' said Hal. 'Apples. At the same time.'

Gilly shook her head. 'I don't like this. We must have missed a seed when I turned my pockets out.'

'A seed from those weird orchards in Vemoria.'

'We found six seeds when we came back. And burnt them.'

'We missed one, then. There must have been seven.'

'They said we wouldn't go back as long as we didn't bring anything from there back with us into our world.'

'Only we did.'

'But we haven't slipped through.'

'Ben has, I'm sure of it.' Hal sounded very definite.

'That's why he said "snow",' said Gilly.

'What?'

'Just before he vanished. I said "fog", and he said "snow". I think he could see through the mist to another place, where there was snow.'

'Sssh,' said Hal. 'Here's Mum back. Any sign of him?' he called out.

Mum came into the kitchen, her cheeks bright with the cold.

'No. I am worried about him; I wonder if I ought to phone the police.'

'They'll say, wait until the fog goes.'

'I suppose so. Oh dear, more disturbance, and I forgot to tell you about the other surprise.'

'Other surprise?'

'Yes, we've got some visitors coming.'

'Visitors? Who?'

'Do you remember Erica?'

'Erica?' said Hal sharply. He gave Gilly a meaningful look. They both remembered Erica all too well. She had visited them the previous summer from America, full of opinions about everything. And she, too, had gone through into that other world, where she had proved to be a dangerous enemy, and on the side of the Vemorians. Gilly and Hal didn't like the idea of her turning up again. Particularly not on a night when this strange fog had appeared.

'What about her?' said Gilly casually.

'I had a phone call from her father. They're over in this country on a trip, and he said could they call in here this evening.'

'And you said yes!' Gilly was horrified.

'Gilly, I know you didn't like Erica very much, but they are family.'

'They are not,' said Hal. 'Distant connections, that's all.'

'Nonetheless, they are coming. So please tidy up the sitting room, while I get on with my work.'

'Why?'

'It's a pit.'

'Not the sitting room, Mum; Erica and co. Why are they coming?'

'I expect they're in this area.'

'Does Dad know they're coming?'

'Yes, of course, I rang him. He's going to try and get home a bit early.'

'I don't suppose he'll try very hard,' said Gilly under her breath, as she dragged the vacuum cleaner out of the cupboard under the stairs.

'What a nerve!' said Hal.

'I really would like to know what Erica's up to and why she's coming,' said Gilly, collecting all the magazines and books which were lying around.

'It won't be to do us any good,' said Hal darkly. 'Here, give me those.' He lifted the lid of a wooden chest in the corner, and tipped everything in. 'There,' he said, sitting on the lid to shut it. 'And I don't like her arriving here when this fog's drifting around and Ben may have slipped through. Too much of a coincidence.'

'Of course they may have to cancel. Because of the fog,' said Gilly hopefully.

'I expect Erica can see through fog. She can do everything else.'

'Infra red vision, probably,' agreed Gilly. 'Of course, we don't know anything about her dad.'

'Bound to be as ghastly as she is.'

'It isn't the ghastliness, Hal. It's that she's *dangerous*. I mean, she's practically a Vemorian.'

'And she thinks we're Tuans.'

'Well, we are, in a kind of way.'

'We aren't,' said Hal fiercely. 'It's nothing to do with us any more. We helped the Tuans to get the Vemorians off their backs, and that was it.'

'I *do* wonder what happened to old talking head,' said Gilly. 'I suppose he did join up with the rest of him.'

'I don't know, and I don't care,' said Hal. 'It was very hairy, the whole business.'

'You wouldn't have missed it, Hal, you know you wouldn't. If we went through again, we could see how Lugh's getting on.'

'No way,' said Hal. 'Absolutely no way am I going back to that world. Come on, Gilly, switch on the hoover. I'll get a duster.'

'I think the fog's lifting,' said Gilly, peering out of the window.

'It would be,' said Hal gloomily. 'Just when we need it.'

'There's still some drifting about, only it's patchy now.'

'We should go and see if we can find Ben,' said Gilly.

'I told you, he's not here.' He gestured to Gilly to keep down. 'There's a car slowing down.'

'Bet it's horrible Erica,' said Gilly, ducking quickly.

'Yes it is, look.' Hal, hidden by the curtain, pulled a rude face. Then he straightened up, aghast. 'Gilly, look!'

The man who had been driving the car got out and shut the door. As he turned to lock the car, his face was lit up by a streetlamp. Gilly and Hal gazed in disbelief at the tall dark man, with the coldest eyes they'd ever seen.

'That can't be Erica's dad,' cried Gilly.

'He's very sinister,' said Hal.

'Don't you recognize him? He's one of the Twelve, from Vemoria. The one who came after us. And he's here, at our house.'

'You're right,' said Hal. 'Quick, out to the back. Now!'

They fled into the kitchen, Hal wrestling with the key to lock the back door behind them. 'Just in case they come looking for us,' he said. They could hear the doorbell pealing as they dashed down the path.

'It'll take Mum a couple of minutes to answer it,' said Gilly. 'She'll think we're going. Now what?'

'Hide,' said Hal. 'Then we can slip out along the passage while they're making polite conversation inside.'

The fog, now much less thick and clammy and more like mist, cleared for a few seconds, and they could see the apple tree with its astonishing winter blossom. Then the tree and its flowering branches vanished in a billowing cloud of mist.

Hal and Gilly dived into the mist. 'This won't hide us for long,' said Gilly, her teeth chattering. 'Mum's bound to come and haul us in.'

Hal wasn't listening. 'Gilly,' he whispered in a startled voice. 'Gilly, it's snowing.'

Gilly blinked. They were still surrounded in soft whiteness, but Hal was right. It wasn't mist any longer. She felt the wetness on her cheeks as gigantic flakes of snow floated down, landing on her face and hands, dropping softly to the ground. She looked down in disbelief. 'Hal, there are inches of snow. It must have been snowing for ages.'

'I know,' said Hal, with a huge sigh. 'Guess where we are.'

'We can't be,' said Gilly. 'We're still in our garden. Here's the tree …' As she looked around with more attention, her voice faded away. Yes, there were trees, but they were different trees, never seen in an English garden. They were no longer in an English winter garden, bedraggled and bare except for the strange, flourishing tree. They were on a hillside, looking out over a patchwork of snow-covered fields, threaded through by a gleaming river.

'Oh, Hal,' said Gilly when she'd recovered. 'It's magical.'

'Unfortunately, that's exactly what it is,' said Hal with foreboding. 'Magical. And I wonder what we're in for this time. And where is Ben?'

Two

BEN GAZED AROUND HIM AT THE SNOW, PUZZLED.
One minute he had been walking along a damp,
grey pavement.

The next minute everything was blotted out by a
thick and dangerous mist.

The minute after that he had found himself here, in
the remote countryside, in the middle of a white
landscape.

He shook his head, took off his glasses and rubbed his
eyes. I'll shut my eyes and count to ten, he thought.
'One, two, three ...'

No good. He was still in this snowy place, alone.
Where were Gilly and Hal? Where was the familiar
street with its houses and their bare front gardens? And
where was the traffic? It was so quiet.

Uncannily quiet.

Ben shivered. He never dressed very warmly, and he
could feel the chill striking into his bones. He zipped up
his jacket and put his hands in the pockets. He was still
cold; in fact, the tip of his nose was so cold he could
hardly feel it any more. He bent down and picked up a
handful of snow. Then he rubbed it on his nose; didn't
that stop you getting frostbite?

It wasn't snowing any longer, and Ben could see for
miles. He looked down a valley, with a river winding
along its floor, and up to the top of the steep hills on the

other side. The sun was shining, which was odd, too, because it had been dusk when the fog had come down.

I've fallen over and hit my head, decided Ben. In a moment, I'll wake up in bed somewhere. Or in an ambulance.

Even while he had these comforting thoughts, he knew they weren't true. He hadn't fallen, why should he, walking along on the pavement? He wasn't hurt, just cold. And he didn't think he was dreaming or hallucinating; there was nothing vague or unreal about this landscape. Different, yes. Unreal, no. Besides, look at the way his specs were misting over. He never wore glasses in his dreams.

He took them off, huffed at them, and rubbed the lenses on his sleeve. That made them smeary, but at least he could see more clearly. He gazed down at the snow. It was scuffed in places, he now saw. Why? he wondered, and knelt down to have a look.

How odd, he thought. They aren't scuffs, they're more like footprints. Well, bird prints, perhaps. And then he laughed. If these were the prints of a bird, the bird would be bigger than an ostrich.

Just the snow falling unevenly, he told himself. Or blown by the wind. Still, it was funny the way they seemed to go in a line. Maybe there was a path under the snow there, and that was why the snow was patterned like that. It couldn't do any harm to follow the line; if it was a path, it would lead somewhere.

Wrapping his arms round himself, and banging his hands against his ribs to try and keep warm. Ben began walking. It was slow, cold work; the snow seemed particularly slippery, and Ben found himself sliding about on it rather than sinking in, the way you usually did on snow. Come to think of it, the snow was a strange colour, with a purply tinge to it, which he had never seen before.

But then I haven't seen much snow, he told himself stoutly. If I'd been skiing, or gone up mountains, I might have seen lots of snow like this. He slipped and slid on, making slow progress, but at least getting warmer with the effort of moving. As he went on, he became more sure that the patterns in the snow were leading somewhere. Otherwise, they'd be all over the place, and they definitely followed on in a regular way.

They *did* look like footprints, though.

Now the path or whatever it was began to go upwards, and Ben found the going even harder. He was tempted to pause, have a rest, but he was still alone in this lonely white world, and he knew from books what happened to people who rested in the snow. So he trudged on, ears and nose tingling, fingers numb, wishing that he was at home. Even the very dull food which his aunt either cooked for him or left out on the table if she were going out and had remembered seemed attractive right now.

Then, to cheer himself up, he thought of the weekends when his mother came down to see him. She came whenever she could, but her job in London wasn't exactly nine-to-five, and she very often had to work in the evenings and at weekends. Ben longed to live with her, and go to school in London, but she would never listen to him.

'Ben, I only have a one-room flat in London, and there'd be no one there when you came home from school.'

Ben could have pointed out that there often wasn't anyone at home now when he came home from school, but he didn't want to worry his mother. He knew quite well that life wasn't easy for her.

'And your school here is much better than the one near me in London.'

Oh, yes? thought Ben. Little does she know.

But it was great when she did come, and they did things together, and she cooked him all the things he liked best, which his aunt would never let him have.

'Sausages? Poison, Ben, poison,' his aunt would say.

Ben loved tomatoes.

'Far too acidic, Ben, they'd do you no good at all.'

'I don't like nettles very much,' he'd once protested when she'd made nettle soup yet again.

'Very good for you, Ben, nettles cleanse the blood. Now eat up, there's many a child would be grateful for a bowl of soup like that.'

No there isn't, thought Ben, trying to drown the taste of the nettles with the tough brown bread which his aunt favoured.

Ben was feeling more and more hungry. I must come to a house or a village soon; this path must be going somewhere, he told himself.

It was. As he reached the top of the hill and followed the tracks along the top, he could just see a building in the distance. It looks like a barn, he thought. And if it's a barn, then there should be a farm nearby. And if there's a farm, there will be people, and a fire, and food.

He struggled on, going too fast in the uncertain conditions, so that he lost his footing and tumbled down the slope which led to the barn. He ended up inches from the side of the barn, a solid, stone-built affair with a tiled roof.

Ben got to his feet, brushed the snow off himself as best he could, and made his way cautiously along the side of the barn. He felt uneasy, and he wasn't sure why. Then there was a crash behind him, and he whirled round, his heart thumping, his mouth dry.

A pile of snow lay on the ground, where it had toppled down from the roof. Ben let out the breath he had been holding and moved on.

Another crash, another heap of snow.

And then another.

Ben stopped. Why should these cowpats of snow be hurtling down from the roof? A gentle slide of snow could be expected. But three? And not coming down as a smooth patch of snow from the tiles, but looking as though someone – or something – had given the snow a good shove.

Definitely uneasy now, Ben backed away from the barn, to see if he could get a proper look at the roof. No, he was too short, the ground too low, the barn too high. And besides, he must be imagining things. Maybe there was a stove of some sort inside the barn. That would melt the snow on the roof.

Wouldn't it?

There was the entrance, wide enough to take a huge cart, piled high with hay, and with two enormous wooden doors set into the doorway. One was ajar, leaving a gap of a few inches. Ben gave a quick glance around, unable to shake off the feeling that he wasn't alone, and advanced stealthily towards the gap.

He peered inside, into the darkness. The light from the door hardly seemed to let in a glimmer of light, and the slits set high up in the walls were mere pencils of whiteness in the gloom. Ben sniffed; there was a fragrance of hay. And of something else, not hay, not animals or the smell of wood and stone. This was a smell of food.

Ben slipped through the door into the barn. Once out of the snow dazzle, his eyes began to make sense of the gloom. He could see a long table set along one end of the barn. And yes, his sense of smell hadn't misled him;

once he got closer he could see that rows of apples were spread out on the table.

Ben hesitated. He had scrumped enough apples in his time, and he was very hungry, and there were a lot of apples. Surely, whoever the barn belonged to wouldn't miss a single apple, one out of so many. Or two even. He stretched out a hand and was just about to pick up an apple when he heard a voice.

'I wouldn't, you know.'

Ben's hand dropped to his side as he peered round. Who had spoken? Who was in there with him.

'I'm up here,' said the voice.

Ben looked up into the network of beams which supported the roof; beams as thick as tree trunks. Who was up there? He couldn't see anyone.

'Over here.'

And there, in a corner, Ben could see two gleaming, unblinking golden eyes. Astonishing eyes, and definitely not human. Ben strained to see more. Who could it be? A cat? Well, if it was, it was some cat, and ...

What am I thinking of? Ben said to himself. A cat, talking! How ridiculous. Yet whatever it was up there, it didn't seem human. And who would be perched up in the rafters like that?

'Who are you?'

'Don't ask questions, I don't like questions,' said the voice.

'Are they your apples? I haven't taken one.'

'No, but you were going to, weren't you?'

Ben said nothing.

'They aren't my apples as it happens. This place is nothing to do with me, I've just come in to get away from that dratted snow, how I hate it. No, as far as I'm concerned, help yourself. I was just warning you of the risks. But it's entirely up to you.'

'Risks? What risk is there in eating an apple? Oh, you mean if I get caught.'

'The danger lies in the apple itself,' said golden-eyes. 'The owners of the apples aren't very friendly to boys like you.'

'They'd mind me taking one?' said Ben. 'Would they miss just one?'

'If you eat an apple, you'll find yourself in the power of those who own this barn, and the apples in it. They aren't ordinary apples. But go ahead, do what you like.'

'What are you talking about?' cried Ben. 'I don't understand what you're saying. In whose power? And just because of an apple? It doesn't make any sense.'

'I'm only trying to help,' said the voice, sounding a trifle huffy now. 'Go on, take a bite of one of those apples. Mind you, you'll find it pretty sour.'

'I like sour apples,' said Ben defiantly.

'And like cotton wool.'

Ben couldn't say he liked the sound of that. But he was dreadfully hungry.

'Best have a good look before you bite, though,' warned the voice. 'These stored apples have a lot of maggots and suchlike in them. Best to dunk the apple in a bucket of water first, see if you can get the creatures out before you bite. What's worse than finding a maggot in an apple?'

'Finding half a maggot,' said Ben with a sigh. 'That's an old joke.'

'But a new experience for you, maybe,' went on the voice. 'I don't know, some people consider that sort of thing a delicacy. I wouldn't know.'

The apples didn't look as appetising as they had done at first. Ben took a step back from where he was standing, and tried to get a better look at whoever it was lurking up in the roof. 'Why don't you come down?' he asked.

'Not I. It's much safer up here. Warmer and quieter, too.'

'Was it you pushing the snow off the roof?'

'I wasn't pushing it, I merely displaced some of it on my way in.'

'How did you get up on to the roof?' asked Ben.

'In the usual way.'

Ben was about to ask what the usual way was when the doors were pushed wide open, sending a stream of light across the dried earth floor of the barn. Ben looked up in alarm; the golden eyes had vanished and there was nothing in the rafters but darkness. Ben drew back into the gloom as two shadows were cast along the ground.

Two shadows. One short and round, the other long and thin.

The shadows of two people.

Three

'HA, AN INTRUDER,' SAID A JOLLY FEMALE VOICE. 'Intruders in the plural, I'd say,' said another woman's voice, this time high and chilly.

'It's a boy,' they said together, as Ben found himself scooped out of his lurking place and into the light.

He blinked, and wriggled to get away from the iron grasp of the stout little woman who was holding him. A sharp poke in the ribs from her companion, who was the tall shadow, took his breath away, and he stood there in front of them, gasping.

'Quite a small boy,' observed the round one. Surprisingly, hers was the high voice. The jolly voice belonged to the tall, spiky one. They both had jet-black curly hair, extremely unkempt and dirty, and sharp, glowing black eyes which were fixed on Ben, to his growing discomfort.

'Stealing apples, I dare say.'

'How many have you eaten, boy?'

'I haven't stolen any apples,' said Ben, regaining his breath. 'And so I haven't eaten any, either. And I'm not a small boy,' he added for his own benefit.

'Saucy, with it,' said fat and chilly, nodding at the tall one.

'Pity, really,' said the tall one. 'It's quicker and easier that way.'

Ben didn't like the sound of that.

'Well, little traveller,' said the smaller one, never letting go of his arm. 'Where have you come from, eh? And what's your name?'

'Ben.'

'Ben? Not much of a name. And you're from the Gonelands are you?'

'What?' said Ben.

'Never mind, never mind,' said her tall friend. 'Are you cold, Ben? And hungry?'

'Yes,' said Ben. 'I am. And you're hurting my arm.'

'What a pity,' said the smaller woman, not sounding sorry in the least, and never loosening her grip. 'You see, we aren't used to boys appearing in our barn, and we think it's better if you don't run away.'

'Where to?' said Ben crossly. 'There's nowhere to go.'

'Nowhere to go? My word, you think you know everything, don't you, you youngsters. Why is there nowhere to go?'

'It's just snow and hills,' said Ben, thinking, what a dim person.

'Is it now?' said the taller one. Her mouth, when she smiled, formed the shape of triangle; not very jolly-looking, really, thought Ben. She swirled across the floor to the wall opposite the big doors, and pointed. 'Did you notice this door?' she asked.

Ben looked hard. 'Is it a door?' he said doubtfully.

'It is,' said the woman, giving it a push from the side.

'Oh, a sliding door,' said Ben, and then caught his breath in amazement.

Where was the snow, the lonely countryside he had trudged through? He looked out over a maze of roofs and windows and little towers. 'It's a town,' he said in disbelief.

The tall woman gave a nasty laugh and slid the door

shut again with a loud bang. 'There,' she said. 'Gone,' and laughed some more.

With a sudden, desperate twist, Ben managed to break free from the tight grip of the other woman. He rushed to the big barn doors and out, into the piles of snow. He ran, sliding and tripping, along the length of the barn to the end. Still snow, still nothing but hills and some trees. He slithered on, round the end to the other side.

No town. No roofs, no towers. Just a steep bank of snow. And behind it, an unbroken stone wall, with no door in sight. It's a trick, thought Ben. The levels must be different. If I can get to the top of the bank, then I'll see the town.

He didn't.

Just more snow, more trees, more hills stretching into the distance. Ben's face darkened with suspicion. Just what was going on here? He slid down the bank and investigated the long barn wall more closely. Not a break in the bricks, no indentations; there was simply no door there. Nothing secret, nothing hidden; it was quite clearly an unbroken wall.

Snow madness, said Ben to himself. The snow and the cold and hunger have affected my brain. I'm imagining all this. It's some kind of hallucination.

'No, it isn't,' said a familiar voice, this time from just behind him.

Ben whirled round. He stared into those weird and wonderful golden eyes, which this time were almost on a level with his. Now, in the light, he could see who the eyes belonged to.

'You're a dragon,' he said, when he finally recollected his wits.

'Yes, of course I am. Didn't anyone tell you it's rude to stare?'

Ben took no notice. How could he help staring at the bronze-scaled creature with its eyes high in its knobbly head, its quite plump body resting on a pair of sturdy claws, its tail coiled up beside it. 'And you've got wings!' said Ben.

'Naturally. How do you think I got on to the roof? Haven't you ever seen a dragon before?'

'No. No, we don't have dragons where I come from.'

'Oh, I expect you do, they probably just keep out of your way. Not surprising if you all crash around the way you do. And why did you give those two your name?'

'They asked me,' said Ben, surprised.

'Tsk, tsk. That's no reason to tell them.'

'Why shouldn't I?'

'The more they know about you, the more power they have over you.'

'Power? Are you nuts?'

'Whatever being nuts is, I'm sure I'm not. Just to equal things out a bit, those two are Ag and Pag. Ag's the tall one, Pag's the short one. In case you run into them again, although it will be much better for you if you don't.'

'Pair of harmless old things like that, what's the problem?'

'Old, yes. Very, very old, in fact. Much older than me, and I was two hundred and sixty-three last birthday,' said the dragon with some pride.

'Oh, come on,' said Ben in disbelief.

'We dragons live for hundreds of years. I've got an uncle who's nearly eighteen hundred years old.'

'You're kidding.'

The dragon blinked at him. 'I am not.'

'Do you get bigger as you get older?' Ben, never having met a dragon before, was uncertain how big dragons usually were, but this one seemed fairly small.

'Of course. Don't you? Huge, I'll be, in about seven hundred years.'

'Oh,' said Ben.

The dragon's mind was back on Ag and Pag. 'Biddies, possibly, although I'm not sure what biddies are. Harmless, definitely not. Those two are Numens. Since you clearly don't know anything about anything, I'll tell you what Numens are. They're a kind of Immortal, and full of nasty powers and malevolence.'

Ben burst out laughing.

'Don't believe me, then,' said the dragon. 'It's entirely up to you. You're a stranger here by the look of you, so I thought you might like to know about things like that. It comes under the heading of helpful advice, you know.'

'I'm sorry,' said Ben. He didn't like the sound of nasty powers, and the dragon didn't seem to be joking after all. 'What powers, exactly?'

'Various,' said the dragon unhelpfully. 'But if you eat any of their food, especially those apples, which, as I told you, aren't ordinary ones, then they would have power over you, and you'd have to do what they tell you.'

'No way,' said Ben definitely. He grinned, thinking of how often he managed not to do what he was told.

'That was back in your world,' said the dragon. 'Things are different here. I was only trying to help, but since you find it all so funny, I'll be on my way.' A pair of wings rose ominously from the dragon's shoulders as he shut his hooded eyes.

'Hey, no, I'm sorry,' said Ben hastily. 'I didn't mean to be rude. It just seemed, well, not very likely.'

'Maybe not where you come from,' said the dragon severely, flashing his eyes open once more, 'but more than likely here. Now in a few minutes those creatures will decide you've been out long enough, and will come to get you. So I suggest we make a move. My name's Tarquin, by the way.'

'I thought you said it was dangerous to tell someone your name.'

The dragon looked at Ben out of the corner of its wild eyes and gave a throaty laugh. 'I don't think you're very dangerous, young man. Now, come along, I haven't got all day. Hold on to my tail, and I'll pull you along.'

It wasn't a comfortable ride. Ben found himself wrapped in Tarquin's very strong tail, and more or less dragged across the surface of the snow. Like skiing, he supposed, only being the ski rather than the skier. By the time the dragon came to a halt, he was bruised and out of breath, and extremely cold.

'We can remedy that,' said the dragon, and blew.

Ben would rather he hadn't. Yes, it was warm air, rather like opening a stove door. But it had a ferocious smell of hot cinders and cooking vegetables and mothballs. 'Thank you,' said Ben, reeling from the blast. 'That's much better, I'm quite warm now.'

'Good,' said the dragon.

'Where are we?' said Ben, looking around and taking stock of his surroundings for the first time. They had come through a pattern of rocks, or standing stones, and behind them was a grassy patch and the opening of a large cave. Ben stared into the half-light within. It opened out beyond the entrance, and as he followed Tarquin, he could see that the cave soared up inside to where he could just make out a jagged roof.

'It's an old dragonslair,' said Tarquin. 'Ag and Pag won't find us here.'

'Would they really try to follow us?'

'Yes,' said Tarquin, rattling the scales on his back in a

disconcerting way. 'Those Numens are ruthless, and don't like giving up their prey.'

Ben wasn't sure that he liked being prey.

'They wouldn't eat you, just make use of you. You're not merely a stranger, are you? You're an Otherworlder, that's what you are.'

'Am I?'

'You look like it. Earth person, at a guess. Why did you come through?'

'I don't know what you're talking about.'

The dragon closed his eyes for a moment, and then opened them again with a flash of gold. 'There are places where you cross from other worlds, such as earth, into this world.'

Ben stared at Tarquin. 'Other *world*? Are you telling me I'm on another planet?'

'No, of course not. You're in another world as far as time and place go. Parallel to yours. There are lots and lots of different worlds all existing at the same time, you know.'

'I did not know,' said Ben, who didn't believe a word of it.

'Some worlds have weak places between them, where people can pass from one to another. Not all of them, but people do pass from your world to ours. And sometimes the other way. In a mist, usually.'

'It was foggy,' Ben conceded.

'There you are then. What we don't know is why you came through.'

'Does there have to be a reason? Isn't it just chance? I mean, I don't believe it, but if it was true ...' Ben thought about his strange journey, and the Numens and the dragon, and his voice tailed away into silence. 'How do I get back, then?'

'Who knows?' said the dragon. 'If we find out why

you came through, then we might have some idea about when and where you could go back. If at all.' He looked at Ben in an intent way. 'Is that a hat?'

Ben put up a hand to feel his skiing hat. 'Yes.'

'Take it off.'

'I like wearing it,' said Ben.

The dragon put out a claw and delicately took the woolly hat from Ben's head. He let out a gentle roar of flame. 'Aha. Red hair.'

Ben stood on tiptoe and tried to snatch his hat back. 'And? he said aggressively. 'What's wrong with red hair?'

'Nothing,' said the dragon. 'A lot of people here have red hair, as it happens. Yours is a very, um, *red* red.'

'What's wrong with that?'

'Striking,' was all the dragon said.

'And while we're on the subject,' went on Ben, 'where exactly are we? I mean, I know we're here in this cave, but what country is this? And what was that town on the other side of the barn? That wasn't there when I went outside.'

'You're in the Thirdlands,' said the dragon. 'Sometimes called the Land of the Gods. Which isn't strictly right, because only part of the Thirdlands belong to the Gods.'

'Gods?' This dragon is crazy, thought Ben.

'The town, which is sometimes on the other side of the barn and sometimes not, is the City of Towers.'

Ben wanted to know more. 'Sometimes? How can a town be there sometimes and sometimes not?'

'The City of Towers is in the Land of the Gods, or, as it's also known, the Thirdlands. Being a place with a lot of Immortals and so on, it's not what it seems, nor are its entrances always in the same place.'

Ben sighed and shook his head. 'This is hopeless.'

'I expect you're hungry,' said the dragon. 'Over there, on the shelf, you'll find some nuts and fruit and things. They're perfectly safe to eat.'

Ben was so hungry he didn't argue, but got himself a large handful of nuts and two big pears. He wasn't too sure about the apples.

The dragon uncoiled his tail and gave it a swish or two and then coiled it up again, very fast. 'Tell me,' he said, 'were you alone in this mist or fog? Or with friends.'

'I was going home from school, with two, well, not exactly *friends*, although Hal is quite friendly ... They're older than me, but they walk home the same way as I do, and I tag along with them. Otherwise there are some types who have a go at me. Then it suddenly got very foggy, and I lost sight of them ... and here I was.'

'The mist is usually there when people come through,' said the dragon. 'I wonder about your friends, though. They may have come through at the same time as you, only to a different place. Or a little later or earlier. One never knows. There's water over there.'

Ben, who had demolished the pile of nuts and the fruit in record time, looked where the dragon was pointing with one huge claw. He went over to investigate, and there, running along the side of the cave between a jumble of stones, was a steady trickle of water.

'It's a stream,'

'Yes. Very handy, don't you think?'

'And slightly fizzy,' said Ben, sneezing as some bubbles went up his nose.

Tarquin sank towards the ground, his legs alongside him, his tail firmly coiled against his side.

'You've changed colour,' said Ben.

'I do that all the time,' said the dragon. 'Depending on my mood.'

'You were a bronze colour outside.'

'That's my action mode.'

'And now you're more blue.'

'That's because I'm thinking. Trying to think, anyway.'

'Sorry,' said Ben.

Silence fell on the cave, as the dragon thought, and Ben tried to pull his jacket more closely about him to keep out the chill, dank air. Tarquin looked up, and breathed out some flames and hot air, which made Ben cough. It did warm the place up, though.

'Best thing is if I take you over the border,' said Tarquin finally.

'Border?'

'Yes. Into Vemoria. Or Tuan, maybe. The Vemorians can be a bit funny about strangers.'

'I'd rather just go home, actually,' said Ben.

'Impossible,' said the dragon briskly. 'That can't be arranged by me or anyone else. Quite beyond our control.'

'I can't stay here,' said Ben, appalled.

'You might have to,' said Tarquin. 'But cheer up, I think it's unlikely. Either you've come over by mistake, in which case you'll find yourself slipping back fairly soon. Or you're here for a purpose, in which case, you won't go back until you've done whatever it is that you've come to do.'

'I haven't come to do anything,' said Ben with certainty. 'It must be a mistake, and all I want to do is get back to Robinson Close.'

The dragon wrinkled his long nose. 'Sounds a bit dull. Still, what you want and what you'll get are two quite different things. They mostly are, you'll find as you get older. Now, we must get going.'

'Where is the border?'

'Across the Spellbound Gorge,' said the dragon. 'And to get there we have to get to the City of Towers. Which isn't always very easy.'

'Why not? Is there a war on, or something? Or is it a long way from here? Don't you have a map?'

'You can't find the City of Towers with a map,' said Tarquin impatiently. 'Not with a *map*. I thought I'd explained. No, no, it's not so easy. We'll have to find one of the entrances, and they move around all the time. Like the one in the barn.'

'I still don't understand. We are talking about the city I saw through the sliding door in the barn? With lots of turrets and stone towers?'

'That's the one. If there's an entrance there at the moment it won't be any use to us. We can't go back or Ag and Pag will get you. And I dare say the entrance has gone. As I said, they shift about a lot. Still, we'll see what we can do.'

Four

'IT'S VERY DARK,' SAID GILLY.

'We're in some kind of cave, I think,' said Hal.

'Smells fusty,' said Gilly. 'I suppose we haven't just wandered into someone's shed at the bottom of the garden?' she added hopefully.

'No,' said Hal. 'What a stupid idea,' he added.

'You haven't a clue where we are, any more than I have, so don't be smug. We should have stayed out on the hillside. I don't like caves.'

'Not a cave,' Hal decided.

'No? So where are we, then?'

'I think this is some kind of passage. A stone passage.'

'Why?'

'If you put your hands out, you can feel walls on either side. And it feels as though it's been tunnelled out.'

'Maybe. But where's the tunnel?'

'Oh, back in Tuan, perhaps. Or Vemoria.'

'Or the Gonelands, or the Thirdlands,' said Gilly gloomily.

'Let's be optimistic and hope it's Tuan.'

Privately, Gilly thought that was a hope on a par with her longing for the physics teacher to have a bad cold every Tuesday, when she had double science. 'And where's Ben? He must have come through as well.'

'Remember last time? The others came through very

soon after us, and from the same place, but they ended up somewhere quite different.'

'True,' said Gilly. 'Anyway, we can't stay here, Hal. We need to find a way out. Can't we follow the wall along? Feeling with our hands?'

'We could be on the edge of a sheer drop, or a step away from a hole going down to a river,' pointed out Hal. 'Think of pot-holers.'

Gilly preferred not to. Caving and pot-holing had never appealed to her for those very reasons. She peered into the thick darkness. 'I can't see a thing.'

'Pity it isn't like the last cave we were in,' said Hal. 'When we could change everything just by thinking differently.'

'I've tried that.'

'So have I.'

There was a faint scuffling and the sound of a pebble rolling along the ground.

'What's that?' hissed Hal, alarmed.

'Me,' said Gilly. 'Sitting down.'

'What's the point of that?'

'If we're just going to stay here, I might as well sit down.'

'Sssh,' said Hal.

'I wasn't making a sound.'

'No, but I can hear something. Listen, it's getting closer.'

Gilly stood up much more quickly than she had sat down, and listened hard. Footsteps, she thought. An animal of some kind? She blinked. She could see a very faint light. And the light was coming nearer.

'It's someone coming this way,' whispered Hal. 'They haven't seen us yet.'

'Oh yes I have,' said a husky voice, right beside them. Gilly jumped. The light was still some way away.

'I put the light down and came to see who was here.'

In the gloom, Gilly and Hal could just make out the figure of a slightly built person. Very thin, in fact.

'Who are you?' said Gilly.

'What are you doing here?' said the man. 'It's forbidden for anyone to be up here.'

'So why are you here?'

'I came up on instructions.'

'Where is here?' said Hal.

'Are you lost?' He sounded curious. 'You must be from the quarry, there's nowhere else you could have come from. Are you trying to escape? You won't get away, you know. Didn't the guards see you?'

'Guards,' said Gilly, her heart sinking.

'Yes, the quarry guards.'

'We didn't see anyone,' said Gilly.

'We've just, well, arrived here,' said Hal. 'Quarry? Are we in Vemoria?' He remembered being told about the slaves on his last visit. Lawbreakers were sent as prisoners to serve their sentences in the quarries. Foreigners taken in battles and others who had wandered across the border were enslaved and some of them, he knew, were put to work in the quarries until they dropped.

'Yes, this is Vemoria. Why? Where did you think you were?'

They could hear the suspicion in his voice. Then he flitted away and was back a minute later, carrying the light and holding it up to get a better look at them.

'Well, you certainly aren't quarry slaves,' he said.

'No, we aren't.'

'No pallor, no dust coating your skin and hair, no swollen eyes.'

Gilly looked at his face, still half in shadow, and realized that he was astonishingly pale, and his skin had an unhealthy grey tinge. 'Your eyes are very red,' she said.

'Yes, the dust gets in them. You go blind in the end, if you stay.'

He said this in such a matter of fact voice that it took Hal a few seconds to realize what he was saying. 'Do you have work in the quarry? Are you a slave?'

'Not exactly,' he said. 'I'm a prisoner. I don't cut and carry the stone, because I'm not strong enough to be much use.'

He turned his head in a quick gesture. 'I must go, or I'll be in trouble. I came in to get something from the stores.'

'Wait a minute,' said Hal. 'How do we get out of here?'

Silence. Then, 'I don't know. At least, I know how you get out of the tunnels, but you'll be picked up by the guards as soon as you come out.'

'Are the guards always there?'

'Until nightfall, when the entrances to the quarry are closed.'

'We'll have to wait until then,' said Hal. 'It can't be long.'

'It's midday,' said the prisoner. 'You'll have a long wait. I have to go. If you want to leave the tunnel, go the way I've come from. First right, second left, and you'll come out into a big chamber. The way out into the quarries is on the other side.' He paused. 'Are you Tuans?'

'No,' said Gilly. 'Not Tuans.'

As Ben watched, the dragon slowly began to change colour again, this time to a yellowy-green shade. 'What does that mean?' asked Ben. 'The new colour?'

'Ah,' said Tarquin, uncoiling his thick tail and flexing

his big and sharp claws. 'That means I'm hungry. Which I am.'

'Um,' said Ben, doubtfully. 'What do dragons eat?'

'This and that,' said the dragon airily. 'What we can find. Whatever's to hand.' He eyed Ben, and a long zig-zag of a tongue swept round the outside of his mouth. 'Not you, you're too small, and you look tough. Besides, I'm feeling fishy today. You stay here, and I'll be back.'

Ben leant against the hard wall, his arms wrapped round his knees. Ben's life wasn't, on the whole, too good, and he often felt miserable. Not now, he realized to his surprise. He didn't feel miserable at all. Just afraid.

Should I clear out? he wondered. While the going was good, and the dragon was out looking for his fish dinner. But how far away was the dragon? And besides, the dragon seemed to be friendly. Which those Numens definitely weren't. Better the dragon you know, he told himself. As long as it went on being a dragon in a fish-eating mood.

Then he began to think how unfair it was that, when he tumbled into another world, he should end up with people after him or threatening him, which was so often the problem in his own world. School bullies, the games master and his aunt there; here those witchy women and Tarquin if he got hungry. Although he was being very helpful, thought Ben, trying to find some reassurance.

He leapt to his feet as he heard a grumbling sound approaching.

Shadows; if he hid in the shadows, he would be safe. Who – or what – was it?

The grumbling sounds echoed round the cave and then stopped, quite suddenly. 'Where are you?' said Tarquin's familiar voice.

Feeling sheepish, Ben came out of his shadowy hiding-place. 'I wasn't sure it was you,' he said apologetically. 'That grumbling noise …'

'Grumbling?' said Tarquin, his scaly brow furrowing, and his eyes snapping. 'Grumbling? I was singing.'

'Oh, I'm so sorry,' said Ben. 'That's what I meant. Only I've never heard a dragon singing before, so I didn't know.'

Tarquin looked distinctly huffy. 'Don't they teach you music where you come from? I would have thought singing was singing anywhere.'

'We don't do much singing,' said Ben hastily. 'At school we do drums, mostly.'

'Drums?' said the dragon. 'I like the sound of that.'

The red colour began to fade back to a bronzy hue, as the dragon squatted, Ben's sins clearly forgiven for the moment. 'We can discuss drumming later,' he said. 'Now we need to make a decision, and we dragons don't find that easy.'

'What about?' said Ben. 'The decision, I mean.'

'I'll explain,' said the dragon, scratching one eyelid with his claw. 'Do we stay here until it gets dark, and then set off to find a way into the city? Or do we go now?'

'If we go now, while it's light, we can be seen,' said Ben.

'Exactly,' said Tarquin. 'So we'd better wait.'

'That's not such a difficult decision,' said Ben.

'No,' said the dragon. 'There's more to it than that. You see, the best time to find one of the entrances is at a transition time.'

'A what?'

'A time of change,' said the dragon mysteriously.

'What kind of change?'

'You know. Noon. Midnight. Dusk. Dawn. Clear

skies to cloud, sun to rain, calm to tempest. And vice versa.'

'So dusk would be good.'

'If we're in the right place,' said the dragon. 'But we might have to travel some way to find it, and in order to be there at dusk, we'd have to travel while it's still light.'

'I see,' said Ben. 'How far do we have to travel?'

'I don't know,' said the dragon. 'We have to find a boundary, and a crossing place of some kind. Like the barn and the door.'

Ben was silent. 'I'm not quite sure I know what you're talking about,' he ventured. 'I remember the barn. Was that special because of where it was, or because it was a barn?'

'Because it was a building at the meeting place of two hills and a stream,' said the dragon. 'Crossroads, that's another likely place. A river with an island. A port, only of course, we're nowhere near the sea. A tower at the forking of the road.'

'It all seems a bit hit and miss,' said Ben. 'How often do you come and go from this city?'

'Practically never,' said the dragon. 'We dragons don't like it much there. It's all very noisy and tawdry, and people aren't courteous to us dragons. My uncle says it's because they're afraid of us, but I think they're laughing at us. Because dragons are rather old-fashioned, you know.'

'I think you're smashing,' said Ben vehemently. 'I don't think you're old-fashioned at all. I think you're the most exciting thing that's ever happened to me.'

The dragon cheered up instantly, blue and gold rippling along his scales.

'Do you? That's excellent. But it still doesn't solve our problem.'

'Dawn, then,' said Ben. 'We could travel by night and

wait at a crossroads, or any other likely place until dawn.'

The dragon shook his head. 'Unfortunately not,' he said. 'We dragons have to fly at dawn.'

'Why?'

'I don't know. We always have, and always will. Dragons fly at dawn. Daily exercise, and we never miss.'

'Then it has to be dusk,' said Ben, who was beginning to feel impatient about the doubtfulness of the whole business. Apart from anything else, he was bored in this cave, and the dragon was probably safer out in the fresh air on a journey. 'Let's leave at once. May I take some more to eat?'

'Help yourself,' said the dragon, waving a claw and unfurling his tail. 'I hope it's the right decision, but stay or go, it's entirely up to you.'

Five

'FREEZE,' HISSED HAL.

Gilly froze, and peered round the jutting rock. Two large figures stood not five paces away from them in the cave, fortunately with their backs turned. They wore the familiar tunics and cloaks of the Vemorians. Both guards had heavily studded metal gloves covering their hands.

They talked together for a moment, in low voices, and then went their separate ways. One disappeared down a dark passage on the other side of the wide cave, while the second one headed for the opening and daylight.

'Now,' said Gilly, and they moved silently along the wall towards the entrance.

They came out on to a wide gallery on top of a sheer drop of stone. Steps were carved in the wall to take you down to the quarry floor, far below, where small figures cut and shaped and heaved slabs of the purple stone. A biting wind whistled round their ears, and Gilly closed her eyes, faint from being on the edge of a precipice. Gilly had no head for heights.

Hal looked at her anxiously. There was no point telling her to brace up. If you got vertigo, then you couldn't cope with heights, and that was that.

'Best get back inside,' he said quickly, taking her by the arm and half-dragging her back inside the cave.

They could hear footsteps; the other guard must be coming this way.

'Sorry,' said Gilly, her teeth chattering with cold and fright.

'Here,' said Hal. 'It's a crevice in the rock, the guard won't see us in here.'

They squeezed in through the crack, elbows and shoulders bruised by the hard stone.

Voices. An angry man's voice, and then a higher voice.

'It's the prisoner,' whispered Gilly.

They could hear the sound of low voices, but not make out what they were saying.

Hal peered round the edge of the rock. 'One of the guards has moved away,' he reported.

'Where's the other one?'

'Standing there, listening to the thin man. He's pointing this way.'

Gilly strained her ears, anxious to catch even a word.

'Tuan,' she said. 'I heard the thin man say Tuan. Hal, I think he's telling the guard about us.'

At that moment, the thin man turned and looked straight towards where Hal was standing. Hal instantly ducked back behind the rock, but the man had seen him.

Hal and Gilly flattened themselves back into a crevice in the rock, holding their breath as footsteps approached.

'Squeeze further in, Hal,' hissed Gilly.

'I can't,' said Hal, and then let out a yelp as he scraped his back.

'Go *on*,' said Gilly.

'There's a hole here,' began Hal, and then he let out a louder shout of alarm, and vanished.

Gilly stood horrified at the side of the dark hole that

had opened in front of her. Then she felt the ground give under her feet, and in a second she was tumbling head over heels and sliding down and down into the darkness.

Ben trudged along beside the dragon. It had started to snow again, and huge white flakes floated gently down from a pinky-grey sky. They landed fatly on Ben's glasses, and he kept rubbing his arm over the lenses to wipe the snow off.

'Why do you wear those?' asked Tarquin, as Ben stopped for the tenth time to breathe on his glasses.

'I can't see very well without them,' said Ben. 'Everything is blurred if I don't wear them.'

'Ho,' said the dragon, puffing a spurt of hot dragon-breath in Ben's direction. 'I expect everything is blurred when you look at it through snow, too. I'd take them off in your position. But of course, it's entirely up to you.'

Ben removed his specs and tucked them into his pocket. The dragon was right, it didn't make a lot of difference. 'Have we got far to go?' he asked, realizing that his feet had got so cold he could hardly feel them any more.

'Difficult to say. There's a crossroads round the next corner, but whether it will be any use or not, I don't know. There could be an entrance there, if we're lucky.'

'At least those Numens won't find us in this snow,' said Ben with satisfaction.

'No?' said Tarquin. 'That's as maybe.'

'They couldn't see us in this, could they?' said Ben. 'And the snow falling must have covered our tracks.'

'You'd think so,' said Tarquin.

'What does that colour mean?' asked Ben with interest, as the dragon's scales took on a dark purple tinge.

Tarquin held up a claw and looked thoughtfully at it. 'Danger,' he said. 'I can feel danger.'

'What kind of danger? I mean, here we are, in the middle of nowhere, nobody in sight, what kind of danger could there possibly ...'

A hideous cackle broke the snowy stillness. 'Got you, got you,' it shrieked.

Ben felt himself gripped by bony, painfully strong fingers. 'Get the dragon, too,' squawked another voice. 'Horrid thing, let's drown it.'

'No, no,' shouted Ben, flailing desperately at the invisible hands which were digging into his shoulders. He felt a great gust of air, and was nearly sent flying by Tarquin's wings as the dragon launched himself into the air.

'How dare you!' roared Tarquin. 'Drown a dragon? I never heard of such a thing. I'm off.'

He soared upwards, and then swooped back to breathe some comfortless words into Ben's ear as he did a final fly-past. 'Forgot to tell you, the Numens are able to make themselves invisible. When they have their silver eyes on.'

With this last, bewildering remark and an extra strong beat of his wings, the dragon flew up into the snow. It was now falling much more heavily, and in a few seconds he had vanished, leaving a stunned Ben in the hands of the Numens.

Gilly landed with a bone-shaking thump which took her breath away.

'Gilly?'

'Oh, Hal, thank goodness you're all right. What happened? Where are we?'

'Goodness knows,' said Hal. 'Ouch, I've hurt my arm.'

'Did you land on it?'

'Yes.'

'If only we had a light,' said Gilly.

'Something fell down when I did,' said Hal. 'I think it may have been the light the prisoner had when we first met him. Scrabble around, see if you can find it.'

Gilly crawled forwards very gingerly in case the ground opened up under her for a second time. She felt around in the darkness, not with any real hope of finding whatever it was that had fallen down with Hal.

'There's a kind of metal box here,' she said.

'That's it,' said Hal. 'Can you open it?'

Gilly lifted the lid. 'There's a little wheel inside.'

'Flick it,' said Hal.

It took Gilly several goes, but then a tiny light flared into life.

'Here's the lantern,' said Hal, who had been groping cautiously around on the ground.

Gilly applied the small blue flame to the wick in the lamp, and blinked at the brightness as it flared up.

'We're on a wide ledge,' said Hal, blinking as his eyes adjusted to the light. 'We must have slid down over there, look, it's some kind of chute.'

It did look rather like the water chute at their local water world, only it was made of hard black stone rather than blue plastic.

'It looks as though it's been made deliberately.' said Hal.

'I expect the hillside is riddled with old tunnels,' said Gilly.

Hal moved his arm and winced.

'It's not much use my offering to look at your arm,' said Gilly, regretting that she'd passed up the opportunity to go on a first aid course. 'I wouldn't have a clue. But we'd better find someone who can help.'

'Back the way we came?' suggested Hal.

'Not with those men up there,' said Gilly. 'And anyway, we can't go back up the chute. It's completely smooth, and there's no way to get a grip.'

'Look down, over the ledge,' said Hal.

'No way,' said Gilly.

Hal dropped on to his stomach, and slithered to the edge. He peered over, and gave a great yell of delight. 'It isn't really a ledge at all,' he said, getting to his feet. 'There are steps cut into the rock.'

'And a sheer drop on either side, I suppose,' said Gilly with a shudder.

'No, it's enclosed,' said Hal. 'Like a spiral staircase, only square.'

'Can you stand up?' Gilly asked.

'Give me a minute or two,' said Hal. 'My head's spinning.'

'Shock,' said Gilly, worried. 'Put your head down towards the ground.'

'That's better,' he said after a minute or two.

'Hal,' said Gilly. 'I know your arm hurts, but I think we'll have to move. Those men will find out where we fell; there may be another way down. They're sure to come after us.'

Hal dragged himself slowly to his feet. 'I'll go first,' he said.

Thank goodness he didn't hurt his leg and he can walk, thought Gilly, as Hal took an uneasy step forward. I hope he doesn't fall. 'Good thing Ben isn't here,' called back Hal, without turning his head. 'It would be awful if we'd landed him in this kind of danger.'

'He's probably back home tucking into his supper,' said Gilly enviously.

Far from tucking into his supper, Ben was worried that

he was going to end up being someone else's supper, judging by the unpleasant way that Ag and Pag were smacking their lips. They'd dragged and pushed him back to the barn, where he now lay in a dejected heap while the ghastly Numens discussed various horrid ideas about his future.

'We can sell him as a slave.'

'Too puny, we'd hardly get anything for him.'

'We could give him to one of the Hroths. They like children.' This suggestion was followed by fiendish cackles from both Ag and Pag, which made Ben's blood run cold.

'Eat him, then.'

'Too small, too bony. No taste.'

Ben breathed a sigh of relief. He'd always minded being so small for his age, but just now he was very glad about it.

'Best thing,' said Ag, in her sharp voice, 'is to make use of him. Send him to find something for us.'

Ben thought it was time he took a part in this conversation. 'I won't go,' he said, sitting up.

Pag gave him a push that laid him flat on his back. 'You'll do just as we say. You have no choice, boy. Because we're going to make you eat something, and then you're in our power, and you have to do what we ask you. A task, a really impossible task. If you fail, you'll be our slave for the rest of your life.'

'For ever,' said Ag happily.

'Not for ever, said Pag, frowning. 'He isn't an Immortal.'

'If he's come through,' said Ag, 'he could be anything.'

'True,' said Pag. 'But he doesn't look like an Immortal, does he? Or even a demi.'

'No,' said Ag. 'Rather a sorry specimen, whatever he

is.' She took one of the apples from the table and advanced on Ben.

He saw what was coming, and clamped his jaw firmly shut.

No good.

Ag was ruthless, forcing his mouth open just like his aunt did when she was making her cat take a pill. I won't swallow it, Ben told himself. I'll hold it in my mouth and then spit it out. They can't make me swallow it.

They could.

They did.

'There,' said Pag triumphantly, as she let him go. 'Wasn't worth making all that fuss about, was it? You should be taught to obey your elders and betters.'

'He won't have much choice, now,' said Ag with an evil cackle. 'What shall we make him do?'

'Something really hard and dangerous,' said Pag. 'Something impossible.'

'There's no fun in that, because he'll give up right away.'

'True.' They looked at Ben, who shrank away under the hard black gaze. Then Pag advanced on him again, and he held an arm in front of his face to protect himself. She put out a stringy hand and snatched the hat from his head.

The two women went absolutely still as they stared at Ben.

'Red hair,' said Ag.

'An Otherworlder,' said Pag.

'Are you thinking what I'm thinking?'

'I'm thinking the Dewstone,' said Ag with a spine-chilling yelp.

'Yes, yes, the Dewstone! Oh, we knew it was going to happen; he's come, just as we knew he would.'

'I expected someone bigger,' said Pag. 'But never mind, he's the one, he's the one!'

Ben watched with apprehension as they clapped each other on the back in a frenzy of gulping glee.

'What will we do with the Dewstone once we have it?' said Ag. 'Always supposing he is the one and he survives, and brings it back.'

More laughter. 'If he isn't the one, then he'll never come back,' said Pag. 'He'll never be seen again, not in this world or his world or any other world, tee hee.'

'And if he is the one, then he can't have it, he's in our power, it's our task, and he has to bring it back for us.'

'The power, the power,' said Pag. 'We can restore the Old Kings.'

'And the Wild Magic.'

'Lots of possibilities,' said Ag with a shriek of evil delight.

She grabbed Ben and held him by the chin, forcing him to look straight into her fearsomely dark eyes. 'Now, listen, boy. This is what you have to do.'

Six

*I*T SEEMED TO GILLY THAT THEY HAD BEEN GOING down the stairs for hours.

Step.

  Step.

    Step.

Six of them. Then a half turn, and six more steps.

Another half turn ...

More steps.

Down,

  ... and down

    ... and down.

They stopped sometimes, briefly, to have a few minutes rest, and to listen hard, as the dull sounds of their footsteps died away. No cries, no clattering feet on the stone, no sounds of pursuit. But just the same, they wanted to go on as fast as they could. It was a strange descent, with guards and enmity behind them and who knew what ahead.

Gilly hated every step. It was with relief that she noticed a difference. 'It's changing,' she said. 'The stone isn't the same.'

'You're right,' said Hal. 'It isn't so black. And it's softer.' He almost stumbled as his foot reached for a step that wasn't there. 'We've reached the bottom.'

'There's a light ahead,' said Gilly.

'A door,' said Hal..

'A very solid door,' said Gilly, catching up with him.

They stood in front of the massive door, made of wood with heavy metal hinges and braces. It stood more than twice Hal's height, and was as wide as a truck.

'We can't open that,' said Gilly.

'We won't have to,' said Hal. 'Look, there's a smaller door set into it.'

'There's a handle here,' said Gilly, turning it as she spoke. She hadn't expected the door to move, but it swung open without a sound. The two of them jumped away from the light pouring in, flattening themselves against the bigger door.

They waited. The door swung gently, but still silently, as though caught by a passing breeze. Chill air blew in, and some flakes of snow.

'I don't think there's anyone there,' said Hal at last. 'I'm going to look.'

They stepped ultra cautiously over the threshold of the small door and into the open air.

It was so dark that at first Hal and Gilly thought it was evening.

'What incredible clouds!' said Hal, looking up into a billowing purple sky.

Gilly shivered and pulled her jacket more closely round her as she looked up at the heavy sky. 'Those clouds are full of snow. We must find shelter, Hal, because it looks like a blizzard's coming.'

'Where do we find shelter?' said Hal.

They had come out on to a steep hillside. Behind them towered the gaunt peaks of black rock, and Gilly stared up at them, unable to believe that they had made their way down through such a mountain.

'Besides,' said Hal, 'we don't know where we are.'

'I think we've come right through the hill,' said Gilly.

'Or mountain,' she added, looking at the huge, dark mass looming over them.

Hal was desperately trying to remember the sketchy map he had seen on their last journey to this world. 'I think the stone quarries are near the border,' he said at last. 'One side of the mountains is Vemoria.'

'And the other?'

'The Gonelands, I *think*,' said Hal, frowning. 'I hope.'

'Where Jouri comes from,' said Gilly. That was someone she'd like to see right now, with his merry face and genius for getting out of tight spots.

'If I'm right,' said Hal, trying to sound positive, 'they probably won't be coming after us.'

'What are the Gonelanders like?' said Gilly. 'I don't remember much about them. Are they into secret police, slavery, rules, that kind of thing? Like the Vemorians?'

'No,' said Hal. 'Jouri told us about them. Makers and craftsmen. Inventors. Engineers.'

His eyes closed for a moment, and Gilly looked at him anxiously. 'Please don't faint, Hal,' she said. 'Is your arm agony?'

'Yup,' said Hal.

'We must do something,' said Gilly.

'Like what?'

'Like not stay here.'

'At least there's some shelter here,' said Hal reasonably. 'We could go back into the mountain, wait for the blizzard to pass.'

'I wouldn't advise that,' said a deep voice from behind them.

Ag and Pag were arguing.

'Send him off as he is,' insisted Ag. 'Let him keep warm as best he can, why should we bother about it?'

'Do you want him just to die of cold after a day or so?' said Pag. 'Chances are, he won't be able to keep himself warm at all, you can see he's not up to much. No, give him a coat, then he's got some hope of getting there.'

'Where's the fun in that?' said Ag.

'Do you want to get your hands on the Dewstone or not?'

Ag thought for a moment, and then looked at Ben, a huddled heap on the floor. 'We know that the Dewstone will be found by a boy with red hair, an Otherworlder, but I'm not sure it *is* this boy. I never saw a more hopeless specimen.'

Pag pursed her dry lips. 'It's worth a try. The signs were all there. And we've never had a boy at all like this in our hands before. Look at his hair! Red? Flaming, I'd say. If he's the one, then there'll be more to him than meets the eye. If not, well, too bad.'

Ag thought for a moment. A crafty look came into her eyes. '*If* he's the one who can find the Dewstone, then he must know he is. Stands to reason. We'll make him tell us.'

'Reason doesn't come into it. There's no reason why he should know. If no one had ever told him about the Dewstone ... and why should they, where he's come from? No, he'll have to find out the hard way. Give him a coat, and turn him loose.'

Ben shut his eyes. 'Yes, please, please do that,' he said to himself, over and over again. Then I can escape, find a way back into the real world.

He was hauled unceremoniously to his feet by Pag, who thrust her face close to his, eyes glinting. 'Don't even think about it,' she snarled. 'That's not the way things work here. You ate our apple, you can't go back to your own world until you have completed the task we have set you. That's the law, and nothing can change it.'

'What law?' said Ben defiantly. 'It's rubbish, there can't be a law like that.'

Pag wasn't having it. 'Listen, scum, this is another world you're in. This is our country, not yours. And our barn, and we're in charge right now. Our country's laws are what govern you, and they aren't written on paper. They are ancient, magic, all-powerful laws, and there's nothing you can do about them.'

She flung Ben away, and he flattened himself into the wall, watching the horrid pair with eyes full of tears of fear and rage.

'You must find the Dewstone,' Pag spat at him, 'which is one of the Stones of Destiny, and you must bring it back to us. And don't ask why, because I've just told you why. You do it because we've told you to do it.'

'What is the Dewstone?' Ben asked.

'A stone, you stupid boy. I assume you know what a stone is?' She leered into his face, and Ben backed away from the waft of foul breath.

'I mean, what kind of a stone,' said Ben. 'Will I be able to carry it?'

'It isn't very big,' said Ag. 'Like this,' she added, holding her hands a little way apart.

Smaller than a football. About the size of a cricket ball. 'Where do I find it?'

That earned him another clout from Pag, although he ducked and avoided the worst of the blow.

'If we knew that, we would have got it long ago,' she hissed. 'There is a map, they say, in the Tower of Troubles. Go to the City of Towers, find the Tower of Troubles, find the map. Got that?'

'No,' said Ben boldy. 'Tower of Troubles? I don't believe it.'

'You'd better believe it,' Ag said in her nasty way. 'It's your only hope.'

'Here,' said Pag. She had a pile of fur in her arms, which she carelessly tossed at Ben's feet.

'A fur coat,' he said. 'I can't wear fur.'

'Wolf,' said Ag. 'Don't wear it, then. Go out in what you've got on, and freeze to death.'

Ben slowly put on the coat. It came down almost to his ankles, although the arms were about the right length. And it was wonderfully warm.

'Poor wolf,' he said softly to himself.

'Poor wolf, nothing,' snapped Pag. 'That wolf and his brother, which is what you're wearing, terrorised three villages before they got turned into a coat. Now, be off with you.'

'It's dark,' protested Ben, peering out through the great doors.

'And so?' Pag gave him a none-too-gentle shove between his shoulders. 'We've had enough of you. Be off, and bring us back the Dewstone. That is, if you ever want to see your family and friends again.'

The door banged shut behind Ben, and he could hear the great metal bolt being drawn across. He hated the barn, but at the moment, he longed to be able to stay there, out of the icy wind and the deep snow.

Still, wishing wouldn't make it happen. What he had to do was get moving, if only to keep himself warm. And I have to find somewhere to shelter for the night, he thought glumly, wondering whether all the inhabitants of this world were as unpleasant and dangerous as the Numens. Tarquin hadn't been, but then Tarquin had scarpered when Ag and Pag had got hold of him; he made no attempt to help me, thought Ben bitterly.

It was no longer snowing, and Ben looked up into a clear sky which was darkening into twilight. To the west, gathering clouds glowed red with the setting sun. It'll be a fine day tomorrow, Ben told himself. Then he remembered where he was. It might mean something quite different here, he thought miserably. And I don't even know if that is the west. And when the stars come up, they could be completely different.

They were.

Ben had decided to walk down the hillside. Partly because it was easier, and he was too tired to think of climbing; partly because his reason told him that there were more likely to be villages or farms in the valley. It became dark very quickly once the sun had vanished below the horizon, no lingering half-light here. But the moon was already up, and nearly full, and one by one, Ben saw stars appearing in the night sky.

He wasn't much of a star watcher in the normal way, but he welcomed the sight of these stars. Strange stars they might be, but stars twinkling in the sky always bring a sense of proportion.

Ben had slithered and stumbled a lot at first, but he struggled on, and reached what seemed to be the side of a field. There, alongside a high and prickly hedge, were signs of a track. The snow there was no easier to walk on, but at least Ben felt he was heading for somewhere, rather than randomly criss-crossing the snowy wastes.

As he trudged on, he thought about the impossible task which Ag and Pag had told him he had to complete.

Ben slipped for the fiftieth time, and landed with a painful thump. If only I had a sled, he thought. I could whizz down here in no time. He got to his feet again, brushing the snow off his furry shoulders. Where was I? Oh, the Tower of Troubles. He must remember everything they had said. There would be a map. And the map would show him which way to go.

'Make no mistake,' said Ag, 'you're in for a long journey.' And she and Pag had cackled with evil mirth.

Thinking hard about what the Numens had said, Ben didn't notice at first that he was being followed. It wasn't that whatever was following him made any noise. Ben was just aware that there was something there, padding behind him. In fact, he thought with rising panic, more than one something.

'Move!' his instinct screamed at him.

Ben moved.

Seven

'You're the forester,' said Hal, looking at the tall man with a rough green cloak hanging from his shoulders.

Just as I remember him, thought Gilly, looking at his one good eye. It had a clear and piercing gaze and no one would give his other eye, so cloudy and unfocused, a second look. 'I thought you were a Tuan,' she said. 'You were in Tuan last time we met you. And you helped us to get back to our world.' Hope showed in her voice. 'Is that why you're here now?'

'Not exactly,' he said. 'I'm usually to be found along borders,' he said, in his deep voice. 'We met in the Wild Forest, which is one of the boundaries between Vemoria and Tuan. Now I'm here.'

'Where is here?' said Hal, holding his injured arm in his other hand.

'At the edge of the Gonelands,' said the Forester. 'You've come through from Vemoria.'

'I knew it,' said Hal.

'I don't like to bother anyone,' said Gilly impatiently, 'but geography isn't important right now. Not when Hal can hardly walk, and we need to find shelter.'

Hal's arm hurt a lot, but he wasn't letting that one through. 'Geography here is important,' he said argumentatively. 'I mean, if we were still in Vemoria, that's a good deal more dangerous than being in the Gone-lands.'

'Gilly is right,' said the Forester, looking at Hal's grey face. 'We need to be on our way.'

'We can't go far,' said Gilly, worried.

'I have a sled,' said the Forester.

They hadn't noticed it before, but there it was, long and functional, with sheepskins piled up on it. The Forester leant over and scooped them aside, gesturing to Hal to get on it.

Hal was reluctant. 'I can walk.'

'Yes, but you'll slow us down,' said the Forester.

Hal gave in, and sat down on the sled. The Forester took the rope and jerked the sled into motion.

'Where are we going?' said Hal, struggling to keep his balance, which was difficult with only one useful arm. Gilly walked behind, beside the sled, keeping an eye on Hal.

'There's a village not so very far from here,' said the Forester. 'Across a frozen lake. It's a good thing it's been so cold, or you would have difficulty crossing. As it is, we can do it on foot. Although it's a long journey on a cold night.'

Gilly's heart sank as she heard these words. Apart from anything else, she was hungry. And then, as they slipped down the final few yards of hill, everything left her mind except the astonishing sight in front of her.

Hal was speechless, too, as he looked out across the shimmering sheet of ice, twinkling with little green and purple points of light.

'When it isn't frozen,' explained the Forester, 'this lake is pale green-blue, from the plants that grow in it. Now there are crystals in the ice and they give it its strange shifting colours.'

It was the most exhilarating journey, that crossing of

the ice. Gilly soon found it was easy to slide as though on skates, and she swooped along with very little effort. The Forester strode ahead with great easy strides, adding a gentle slide to each step to carry him further across the surface.

Hal drew the fleeces more closely about him; he was very cold. 'Does the lake freeze like this every winter?' he asked, his cheeks bright from the chilly air and the movement.

'Very seldom,' said the Forester. 'Some years it freezes round the edge, and a little way out from the shore, but that's usually all. This is a very cold winter, though. Even the outermost parts of the Thirdlands is deep in snow, and that rarely happens.'

'Why not?' asked Hal.

'Because the Gods, among others, live in the Thirdlands, and the endless summer of their part keeps the rest of it warm. Usually. But, not as I said, this winter.'

Ben knew all about the snow and ice in the Thirdlands, as he was doing an amazing slide on a sheet of frozen mud. He was completely out of control when the shape loomed up in front of him, and there was no way he could stop. He hurtled into it, winding himself in the process.

'Well, really,' said a familiar voice. 'You've disarranged all my scales on that side. Carry on, though, come at me like a cannon ball, I supposed one gets used to it after a while.'

'Tarquin,' said Ben, still rather breathless. 'Oh, I am glad to see you.'

Tarquin turned his head and looked at him with a twinkling golden eye. 'You *say* you are. However, you weren't thinking very well of me not so long ago.'

'No, I wasn't,' said Ben, glancing anxiously behind

him to see if his pursuers were coming after him. 'Because you abandoned me, you know.'

'I did no such thing,' said the dragon. 'I merely decided on the best course of action, and left. I couldn't do much to help you then, and besides, we dragons don't care to get mixed up in these affairs. Very troublesome they usually are. But if you want me to go now; if you're going to bear a grudge, then I'll be off. It's entirely up to you. I merely thought you might be glad of some help.'

'No, no, don't go,' said Ben hastily, grabbing the nearest bit of dragon which happened to be the base of one of his wings.

'Don't do that,' said the dragon. 'It tickles.'

Ben wasn't paying attention to the dragon. 'There they are again, I can hear them,' he said in tones of alarm. 'Listen. They must have come after me.'

'Who's after you? Those Numens? I doubt it, not once they've sent you on your way. Or on their way, to be strictly accurate. And if they were after you, they would have caught up with you by now. Well, you saw for yourself that they're pretty nifty operators.'

'No,' said Ben. 'Oh, quick. I don't know who or what they are. Oh …'

His voice rose in a wail as three great shadowy shapes loped into view. They bounded closer, and Ben clung to Tarquin.

'What on earth's the matter?' said Tarquin tetchily. Ben, who had put up his hand to shield his eyes, peered cautiously out, and found himself facing three huge grey cat-like creatures. They *are* cats, he said to himself in astonishment. Nearly as big as panthers.

'Tsk, tsk,' said Tarquin. 'Pull yourself together. These are Dollops. They won't harm you.'

Ben looked doubtfully at the large pair of fangs visible

on each grey mouth. On the other hand, their big grey eyes looked friendly. 'What wonderful whiskers,' he said, noticing that they, too, were a dark grey colour.

A great rumbling sound went up.

'They're pleased,' said Tarquin.

'They're purring!' said Ben in astonishment.

'Cats do.'

'Why were they chasing me?'

'Curiosity,' said Tarquin promptly. 'Dollops are very curious creatures. Nosy, you might say. They have to know what's going on, especially if there's anything unusual afoot. And an earth visitor running through the snow in the dark is definitely unusual.'

The biggest Dollop seemed to nod his head, and its long tail swished across the snow.

Ben couldn't help laughing. 'It's almost as though they can understand,' he said.

'They can,' said the dragon. 'Telepathy, you know.'

Ben was feeling better.

On the minus side, he was still in the snow, with no house or village in sight, no food, no way of returning to his own, proper home, and with an impossible task ahead of him.

Then there were the pluses.

He was warm.

He had met up with Tarquin again.

And he had to laugh, because these big furry Dollops were so friendly, and because, caught up in an infectious madness, they were now rolling about in the snow like kittens. The biggest Dollop was on its back, taking mad swipes with huge paws at the snow it was throwing into the air. The other two were chasing their tails in a grey whirl of fur and tails.

Tarquin sniffed, and then coughed a smoky cough and gave a sulphurous belch. 'It's bad for us dragons to sniff,' he said. 'It's all very well you standing there, laughing, but this isn't getting us anywhere.'

Ben stopped laughing, and the Dollops became grave and serious beasts. The biggest one looked intently at Ben, and he felt a strange sensation in his brain, out-of-focus pictures flashing across his inner mind as though it was a cinema screen.

Then the Dollop's attention turned to the dragon.

'He's going to come with us,' said Tarquin.

'Come where?' asked Ben.

'Wherever it is you're going,' said Tarquin. 'I can't say I approve, but whether I do or not, it won't make any difference.'

'Why not?'

'Once a Dollop has an idea in its head, it sticks,' said the dragon. 'Tiresome really. They aren't terribly bright, you see.'

The chief Dollop batted at the snow and yawned, showing a very fine set of curved teeth.

'I'd love the Dollop to come too,' said Ben. 'I've got to find something, and I'm not quite sure exactly what it is. And I certainly don't know *where* it is. So I need all the help I can get.'

'I would have thought I could be extremely helpful,' said the dragon. 'Still, if you think my help isn't enough, then it's entirely up to you.'

His scales had turned a dark red colour, Ben noticed with alarm. 'Cats where I come from are very useful at some things,' he said quickly. 'Earthy things, that is, not clever things.'

'Mmm,' said Tarquin. 'I'm not convinced. I can't believe that we're going to be taken seriously with a Dollop alongside us ... Oh, very well, I won't say any more. Send your friends away,' he said to the Dollop. 'And make sure that they know they mustn't tell anyone they've seen me or Ben here, or that you've gone off with us.'

The Dollops bumped noses, and made growling noises at each other. The two smaller ones peeled off and loped away towards some bushes; the remaining one sat with its paws sticking out, looking expectantly at Tarquin and Ben.

Ben wasn't laughing any more. 'What do we do now?' he said. 'Where do we go?'

Another fuzzy image came into his mind, and then sharpened into a picture of the city he had seen through the barn door.

'The City of Towers,' he said, surprised. Then the picture faded, and a flash of winding road swam into his mind. A cottage, with what seemed like a lot of chimneys. Then that, too, faded.

Tarquin raised a claw in a thoughtful way. 'I know where that cottage is,' he said. 'Not far from here. I wouldn't have thought ... Still, it's worth a try. These Dollops may be dim when it comes to basic reasoning, but they're good on this kind of thing. Of course,' he added, giving Ben a cold look, 'you may prefer to try elsewhere. It's entirely up to you.'

'No, no,' said Ben. 'We'll go where you think best.'

'This way, then,' said the dragon, raising the scaly spikes above his eyes as the Dollop leapt ahead of them, full of bounce. 'I think this may be an interesting trip.'

Eight

*T*HE EXHILARATION OF THE SILENT AND MAGICAL journey across the ice gave way to cold feet, a rumbling stomach and a tiredness so complete that Gilly could hardly move her arms or legs as they came down a frozen path towards a cluster of stone houses.

Surely no one's there, thought Gilly, looking at the dark windows as the Forester stopped in front of one of the houses and gave three short raps on the door.

Her heart leapt. Surely that was a noise from inside the house? She glanced at Hal as he scrabbled uncomfortably off the sled to stand on unsteady feet. He had heard something as well. Then there was the unmistakable sound of bolts being drawn back and the squeak of a key turning in a lock.

The door swung open and light spilled out on to the snow. A figure stood there, a shadowy outline against the light from inside. The Forester spoke a few words in a low voice, and then the person who had opened the door beckoned to Hal and Gilly. 'Come in, come in out of the cold, it's a bone-chilling night,' he said, leading them along a narrow passage.

I know that voice, thought Gilly in disbelief. And at the same moment, Hal let out a whoop of joy. 'Jouri,' he cried. 'Jouri, it's you!'

There was no more to be said for a while, as Jouri,

refusing to answer any of their questions, bustled about. 'First, let's look at your arm, Hal,' he said.

Some excruciating moments later, Jouri pronounced himself satisfied that the arm wasn't broken, just badly bruised. 'I've got something that'll take the pain and the swelling away,' he assured Hal. 'I'll see to that first, and then we'll eat.'

Gilly almost protested, she was so hungry, but a look at Hal's face, and the words died on her lips. And in a minute she was busy helping Jouri as he expertly cleaned the broken skin and smeared a colourless but pungent ointment on.

Jouri hadn't changed at all, thought Gilly as she watched him putting a bandage on. He was just the same, a wiry, lively, small man, always smiling, but with wickedly intelligent eyes that missed nothing. Gilly knew he was a spy, who risked his life travelling in Vemoria to send information and news back to Tuan, Vemoria's weaker and threatened neighbour. Other than that, she knew little about him.

An hour later, they sat warm, well-fed and sleepy round a crackling log fire in the big, stone-flagged room which served as a kitchen and sitting-room. Hal was half-asleep, but there were some questions Gilly was longing to ask. 'Is this your house?'

'I spend a lot of time here when I'm not on my travels,' said Jouri, evasive as ever. 'It's my sister's house, but she isn't here at the moment. She's a wonder with brews and potions, that drink I gave to Hal is one of hers.'

Yes, thought Hal, wrinkling his nose. The strong, bitter, herby smell still lingered.

'No point feeling pain when you don't have to,' said Jouri.

Hal yawned and stretched out his legs, watching the fire dancing in the grate.

'You're growing,' said Jouri.

'Not much,' said Hal sleepily. 'It hasn't been long, only since the summer.'

'Twice in one year you've come through from your world.'

'Twice in four months, actually,' said Gilly.

'So what brings you two back?' said Jouri. 'That's what I want to know.'

Hal yawned, and clapped a hand over his mouth. 'Sorry,' he said. 'The fire's making me sleepy. It's no good asking us; we haven't got a clue.'

'Yes, we have,' said Gilly. 'You had that strange dream, about Ben being lost, and about being here again. And I think it's something to do with that apple tree in the garden.'

'Apple tree?' Jouri didn't seem very surprised. 'You took something back with you, after all, did you? Seeds? Oh, very unwise. That would leave an opening between the worlds, which would make it very easy for you to slip through again. And it would mean that some people here would know that there was a possible way through to your world ... It could be interesting.'

'It was a mistake,' said Hal. 'They were in Gilly's pocket. We thought we'd burned them all.'

'We did burn all the ones we found,' added Gilly.

'One must have fallen on the ground where we couldn't see it,' went on Hal.

'Was there anything special about this tree?' asked Jouri.

'It was blossoming in the middle of winter, for a start,' said Hal. 'And it's got apples growing on it as well.'

'That's one of the trees from the orchard of the Old

Kings all right,' said Jouri. 'They're the only apple trees I ever heard of that bloom and fruit at the same time. It would make a place for you to slip through, no question of that, there's powerful magic in those apple trees, as you found out last time. But why now? And why here?'

'Ah,' said Hal. 'The tree wasn't the only thing. There was a fog, wasn't there, Gilly? And Erica tipped up on our doorstep. Do you remember her, Jouri?'

'I do,' said Jouri, his smile vanishing for a moment.

'With that terrible, dark, grim man who was with her then. One of the Twelve.'

That really did make Jouri sit up. 'What? In your world? Surely you're mistaken.'

'No, we're not,' said Gilly. 'You couldn't mistake him, not with him being so tall and so evil-looking and altogether memorable.'

'It's not the first time he's been in our world, either,' pointed out Hal. 'He chased us when we'd just got back through last time.'

'Our mother thought Erica was coming with her dad,' said Gilly. 'So I don't know why this guy was with her. I mean, he can't *be* her father, not when he's a Vemorian.'

Jouri frowned. 'I wonder,' he said, lapsing into silence.

'What happened after we went?' asked Gilly after a while. 'Where's Lugh?'

'He's in the Walled City,' said Jouri, his mind still elsewhere. 'Studying to be a full soothsayer. Although just at present ...'

'And Tuan?' Gilly persisted. 'No more raids from Vemoria?'

Jouri shook his head. 'Vemoria has its own problems right now. Once they're settled, I wouldn't be surprised if they didn't get up to all kinds of mischief again.'

'Problems?' said Hal.

'There's strife among the Twelve who rule Vemoria, so people say. It may be just rumour, and I don't think it amounts to much, but it's a sign that there may be trouble stirring further afield. Not this year, or even the next, but then ...' He shook his head. 'The Twelve aren't feeling so safe any more. And they've felt utterly secure, oh, for centuries.'

'If the Twelve are in trouble, it's good news, isn't it?' said Gilly.

'Good news for some,' said Jouri cryptically. 'Who called you, that's what I want to know. And why?'

'Does there have to be a reason?' asked Hal. 'I thought it was because of our having taken the seeds with us. The Forester warned us not to take anything from this world back with us, or we could be drawn back again ... They were in Gilly's pocket.' Hal paused, and he looked around the room. 'Hey, where is the Forester?'

'He's gone,' said Jouri.

'He can't have,' said Hal. 'He was here just a minute ago.'

'He slipped out,' said Jouri.

Gilly was alarmed. 'On a night like this?' The threatened blizzard had arrived a short time after they were safe indoors, and they could hear the rising wind shaking the doors and shutters.

'He'll be safe,' said Jouri.

'I do hope Ben isn't out in this,' said Gilly.

'We don't even know if Ben came through,' said Hal reasonably.

Jouri gave him a very sharp look, and sat up. 'Ben? Who is this Ben? Was he with you?'

'Not exactly,' said Hal.

'He was walking home with us,' explained Gilly.

'When it got foggy. He vanished, we looked around for him, but there was no sign of him.'

'And then you found yourselves here?' asked Jouri.

'No,' said Hal. 'That was later. Quite a bit later. We'd nipped out to the garden because of Erica and that dark man.'

Jouri was now very alert indeed. 'So, if this Ben came through, it wasn't at the same time? Or in the same place?'

'No.'

Jouri let out a long breath. 'What does he look like, this Ben?'

Gilly told him. 'Small with specs.'

'An ordinary kind of boy?'

Hal and Gilly couldn't answer that immediately.

'He gets bullied a lot,' said Gilly finally. 'Because his classmates find him strange.'

'They call him sad. Weird,' said Hal.

'You don't share their opinion?'

Another pause.

'Not really,' said Hal. 'He's different, it's true ... But there's something about him.'

'Yes,' said Gilly. 'He's different. And difficult. And of course his hair doesn't help.'

'Hair?'

'He has red hair. Really red, blazing. They go on at him about it.'

'Now this,' said Jouri, 'changes the whole thing. This is extremely interesting.'

'Is it?' said Gilly. 'Is Ben here, in this world, do you think?'

'I'm sure he is,' said Jouri. He stood up, rubbing his hands briskly together. 'Bed, now. Get all the rest you can, because as soon as the snow's stopped, we'll be on the move.'

'Typical,' said Hal as they went up the steep stone staircase. 'Just as soon as we get somewhere comfortable, we have to be off.'

'Would you rather not go?' asked Gilly. 'Is your arm still hurting?'

'Hardly at all,' said Hal, looking at it in a surprised way. 'Whatever Jouri put on it works very well. If it's still like this in the morning, I'll be fine to go anywhere he wants.'

'And we don't know where that is,' said Gilly. 'I hope it isn't Vemoria, with those Watchers and Wardens all over the place.'

'I hope it's a journey to a patch of mist and straight back home,' said Hal, yawning.

'Ben may be in danger,' said Gilly, stopping to admire the carving of a dragon's head at the top of the stairs.

'Bother Ben,' said Hal.

Clearly Dollops had special powers. Even Tarquin had grudgingly to admit that the Dollop had done well.

It had seemed to Ben to be an ordinary cottage, if of an unfamiliar style. Like something from a travel poster, he decided, what with the pink walls and the steep roof. Not to mention those eight chimneys, which seemed a lot for so small a house.

Only it wasn't at all small inside.

'Right time of day,' said Tarquin. 'Dusk. Don't knock,' he added quickly, as Ben approached the front door. 'If this is the right place, then the door will be open. And no one would answer your knock, in any case.'

The door opened into a huge hallway. Ben was startled. 'It looks so tiny from the outside,' he said.

'That's just a façade,' said Tarquin, his claws setting

up a mighty clatter on the tiled floor. The Dollop, on the other hand, wasn't making a sound as he padded on big soft paws, tail twitching, whiskers forward.

'How do we know which door we should try?' whispered Ben, and then jumped as the echo of his whisper hissed back at him.

'No need to whisper,' said Tarquin in what seemed to Ben to be an unnecessarily loud voice. 'The Dollop will know.'

The Dollop had better, thought Ben. The long hallway was lined with doors, Ben could count a dozen at least. And, by the look of it, there were more leading off the curved staircase which led up to a higher floor. And still more along the galleried landing at the top.

'Do all these doors lead into rooms?' he asked Tarquin.

'Oh, no,' said Tarquin. 'Don't forget, we're in the Thirdlands here. The Land of the Gods. Open one door and you'll find yourself a thousand years ago, open another, you could be a thousand miles away ... Risky business, getting into the City of Towers, I told you that.' He gave Ben a scaly look. 'Of course, it doesn't bother us dragons, but if you're nervous about it, don't try any of the doors.'

'Then where would I be?'

'Here, I suppose.'

'I think we'd better try and find the right door.'

'It's entirely up to you.'

Ben was about to reply when some grey thoughts wafted into his mind. The Dollop was sending a message. Several messages, judging by the muddle which seemed to be coming through.

'Eh?' said Ben, confused.

'Concentrate,' said the dragon severely to the Dollop.

'That's the problem with these Dollops, they do get distracted. Towers, Dollop, the City of Towers.'

'I'm getting a rat,' said Ben in sudden fright.

'I expect the Dollop's hungry,' said the dragon. 'Ah, wait a minute, I think he's found it.'

The Dollop had taken up a crouching position in front of the fourth door on the left, and he opened his mouth to let out a gentle roar at Tarquin and Ben.

'Is it the right one, do you think?' asked Ben. 'Or is there a rat on the other side?'

'Let's see,' said the dragon. 'But first, take off your coat.'

'I'll freeze.'

'Not in the City of Towers, you won't. You don't catch Immortals and demigods putting up with all this wintry chill. Leave it here, and then you can open the door.'

'Who, me?'

'You,' said Tarquin firmly.

Nine

WARMTH. THAT WAS WHAT STRUCK BEN FIRST, AS he nervously pushed open the door a tiny crack.

'Go on,' said Tarquin impatiently. 'Once you've opened the door, you have to go on. You can't shut it now.'

A firm push from the dragon's foot was enough to send Ben hurtling head first into the City of Towers. He landed on his hands and knees, much to the delight of the Dollop, who gave him a warm lick of encouragement.

'Ouch,' said Ben, wincing as the tongue rasped over his cheek.

'What are you doing down there?' Tarquin enquired unhelpfully.

Ben's head felt strangely light as he hauled himself upright and looked around. There had been a familiar feel to the snowy landscapes he had found himself in before, but this place was completely different.

It really is another world, thought Ben, looking round with a sense of awe. They were in a corner of a huge piazza, with colonnades all round, and a complicated pattern marked out in dark blue tiles across its shadowy central part. Streets led off it like spokes from a wheel, and Ben could see more colonnades and interesting looking houses with exotic curves and wavy bits to them. Brightly coloured, too; quite unlike anything he had ever seen in his life.

And towers. Round towers, square towers, octagonal towers, towers soaring up into spires. Every house had its turrets and towers, each one brightly coloured, some with sparkling windows, some with flowers tumbling down, some with little galleries running round them at different levels.

His head spinning from the exotica all around him, Ben returned to more practical matters. 'Where's the snow gone?' he asked.

Tarquin had rattled all his scales so that they stood out, making him look bigger and more impressive. 'Snow?' he said. 'Here? In the City of the Gods? Where demigods and Immortals live?'

'I didn't know,' said Ben helplessly. 'But how can it be snow there where we've just come from, and warm like a summer's evening here?'

'Magic,' said Tarquin briefly. 'Now, keep your head down, walk confidently, and get out of the way quickly if someone's coming the other way, or wants to pass you.'

'Why?' said Ben, not liking the sound of that.

'Because they may be powers of one kind or another, and you can't argue with them.'

'And you're going to let them push you out of the way?'

'I,' said Tarquin haughtily, 'am a dragon, an Ancient One, or at least I will be in due course. No one pushes us dragons around. You, on the other hand, are a boy from another world, not immortal, not powerful, and not important. So watch your step.'

A fuzzy image from the Dollop inched its way into Ben's mind. He couldn't make any sense of it, but it made him feel dizzy all over again.

'Ah,' said the dragon, looking at the Dollop. 'The

Dollop thinks you *are* important. Well, Dollops are dim, we all know that. Come along, unless, of course you want to stay cowering here until an Immortal thinks he'll borrow you to add to his household. I'm going this way, but it's entirely up to you.'

'Wait for me,' said Ben, as Tarquin set off at a good pace between the colonnades, his tail sweeping grandly from side to side as he went.

The dragon ignored the principal streets, and dived off into a little alleyway before they reached the other side of the piazza. No beautifully decorated houses here, noticed Ben, but tightly packed, densely built houses with heavy beams and timbering. They were so close together at the top level that you could lean out and shake hands with your neighbours across the way. Washing hung on lines stretched over the street. This made Ben feel more comfortable, somehow. There might be gods around, but washing was normal, everyday.

'Why is it different here from the other part?' said Ben, panting, when he managed to catch up with the dragon.

'This is the quarter for mortals,' said Tarquin. 'Of course we dragons keep our own ways, and can go anywhere, but you can't.'

'What about the Dollop?'

'Oh, they won't take any notice of a Dollop,' said the dragon airily. The grey tail swished, and Ben got a crunchy feeling in his brain. 'They're rare, so they don't realize what Dollops can do,' went on the dragon. 'That's why he'll be so useful.'

'I can smell food,' said Ben, as they turned a sharp corner. 'Oh!'

They were in a marketplace which teemed with life, in contrast to the shadowy, deserted passageways they had just walked along. There were stalls selling pots and pans, clothes, flowers, fruit and vegetables – some familiar, and others decidedly new as far as Ben was concerned. One stall was full of parrots; another sold fish swimming in huge glass jars. Cooked food stalls were doing a good business as people milled around to buy their suppers, and more mouth-watering smells reached Ben's appreciative nose.

'I've got some money,' he said, looking doubtfully at the few coins from the bottom of his pocket.

The dragon took a quick look, and waved his head from side to side. 'No good at all,' he said. 'Gold and silver here.'

'Then I'll starve,' said Ben unhappily. 'And where are we going to sleep?'

'Leave it to me,' said Tarquin, making his way to a stall where a man was just putting some chickens on a spit to roast. 'Run out of cooked birds? Losing custom?' he enquired.

The stallholder eyed the dragon cautiously. 'Maybe I am.'

'Want some help?' asked Tarquin. He didn't wait for an answer, but his scales changed from bronze to a dark-purple colour. He opened his mouth and flames spurted out in a red and golden arc.

The stallholder jumped back as the dragon breathed over the spits, which whirled into action from the strength of the blast. The flames licked over the spinning spit and the food began to sizzle merrily. The stallholder sprang to his jars to cast some seasonings over the fast roasting poultry. Delicious smells rose into the air, and a small crowd gathered round expectantly.

'I've got some fish here,' said the stallholder, rapidly threading several large and ugly fish on to another set of spits. 'If you would care to …'

'Two chickens and all the fish heads,' said Tarquin.

'Done,' said the man, unthreading two well-cooked chickens as he watched his fish cooked instantly in a few more puffs of dragon fire. He deftly cut off the fish heads and tossed them to the Dollop.

'Take some chicken,' said the dragon, as they walked on. The Dollop was still at the stall, crunching the fish heads.

'I couldn't eat all that,' said Ben.

'Try,' said the dragon, popping a whole chicken into his mouth. He gave a polite belch. 'Not bad,' he said. 'For a snack.'

'Mmm,' said Ben, realizing how hungry he was.

'And now,' said the dragon, 'we must find the Tower of Troubles. I suppose that's where you're heading for?'

That stopped Ben in his tracks. 'How do you know that?'

'We dragons,' said Tarquin loftily, 'know a great deal. And the Dewstone, which those horrible hags have sent you to find for them, is of particular interest to us dragons. Now, I'm not going to say anything more for now, so eat up your chicken.'

Ben enjoyed every mouthful, but then he suddenly felt so tired he could hardly take another step. He blinked at the dragon, and yawned so widely that he almost choked. 'I'm sorry,' he said. 'I'm very sleepy.'

A longing for sleep, for deep and undisturbed sleep, floated into his mind. The Dollop, who had caught up with them, joined in the yawns, revealing a pink if fishy tongue and an excellently sharp set of teeth.

'That's the trouble with Dollops,' said the dragon severely. 'And, obviously, with Otherworlders as well. We dragons can go a long time without sleep.'

Bully for you, thought Ben rebelliously. He was so exhausted, he felt he could lie down there, on the cobbled street, and sleep for hours.

The dragon sighed. 'This way, then,' he said. 'And I trust that this wasted time doesn't turn out to spoil our quest.'

'Where are we going, and why?' said Hal, his breath making little clouds in the chilly air.

'To the Land of the Gods,' said Jouri. 'The Third-lands.'

'Why?' said Hal. 'Why should we go anywhere at all? All I want to do is find Ben, and get him home.'

'Ben's in the Thirdlands,' said Jouri.

'How do you know that?'

'It's my job to know about everything that affects Tuan.'

'And how can Ben have anything to do with Tuan?'

'Take it from me, he does.' Jouri could see that Hal was going to argue. 'All right, if you won't listen to me, then just come with me for now. We're going to meet an old friend.'

Hal was suspicious. 'You don't mean the talking head, do you?'

Jouri laughed. 'Ril? No.'

'Is that his name?' asked Gilly, interested. 'He never said what he was called.'

'No, he wouldn't. Names can be dangerous. No, I don't know where Ril is, up to mischief somewhere, but it needn't bother us.'

'It's Lugh,' said Gilly, looking at Jouri's face.

'Yes.'

'You said he was studying in the Walled City,' said Hal, who liked to be precise about these things.

'He is. But it so happens he's in these parts. I reckon he got word something was up, and you might be coming through. It's his job, after all.'

'Of course,' said Gilly. 'He's a soothsayer.'

'Going to be very good one day,' said Jouri. 'And he

sent a message last night, after you two were in bed, that he must see you. So we need to get a move on; it'll be slow going on the snow. Gilly, you can give me a hand. Not you, Hal, not with that arm.' He dived down the side of the house, and Gilly struggled through the snow after him.

'I'm very wet,' she said, as he handed her some roughly cut wooden skis.

'Soon dry off,' said Jouri. 'And I've got some fur-lined jackets for you and Hal.'

Gilly paused for the fiftieth time to adjust her ski. Neither she nor Hal knew anything about skiing. They had once gone to the dry ski slope in a nearby town for a session; that, they had quickly discovered, was quite different from this push and glide on short, narrow skis.

'It's cross-country skiing,' Hal had said as they slithered about trying to get the hang of it. 'It's quite easy, really.'

Easy, yes, but very, very hard work, thought Gilly. However did Jouri do it, mile after mile, effortlessly?

'I'm used to it,' said Jouri. 'We get some snow every year in Vemoria, and in Tuan and the Gonelands, and I'm always on the move.'

'Where's your donkey?' asked Gilly, finding a handy rock to sit on while she rubbed her sore feet.

'I don't use her much in the winter,' said Jouri.

'How do you carry your samples?' asked Hal. He knew perfectly well that Jouri's samples were only a cover for his real work as a Tuan spy.

'On my back,' said Jouri, sliding forward again as Gilly wobbled to an upright position. 'We haven't got far to go now.'

'Where are we meeting Lugh?'

'In a hut, on the border with the Thirdlands,' said Jouri. 'He doesn't want to be seen.'

Hal felt a prickle of danger down his spine.

'Arm hurting?' asked Jouri.

'No,' said Hal. 'I can see trouble coming, and I just wish I was at home watching TV.'

'You wouldn't be,' pointed out Gilly. 'On the way home you said you had a pile of homework.'

'True,' said Hal with a sigh. 'And when we get back, it'll still be waiting for me, if it's the same as last time. Or, if I'm unlucky, it'll be an hour or so later and bedtime, and no homework done and up at six o'clock to finish it before school.'

'Look on the bright side,' said Gilly. 'We might go back and find ourselves in another time.'

'Great,' said Hal. 'Mum would really appreciate that.'

They glided across the snow towards the hut, snow-covered and isolated in a spot beneath high mountains. The door to the hut was low, and even Gilly had to duck to get in. She went first, eager to see their friend from last time. Lugh was a Tuan, whose family and village had been threatened by invading Vemorians. It was he who had set them off on their impossible task of carrying the talking head to the other part of Tuan.

'Just the same,' said Gilly.

'Hello, Lugh,' said Hal.

'I never thought I'd see you again,' said Lugh. 'It was hard saying goodbye to you, and now, here you are once more.'

'Don't ask us why,' said Hal.

'No, Hal,' said Lugh, as Jouri shut the hut door. 'I'm going to tell you why.'

Ten

*L*UGH DIDN'T SAY MUCH ABOUT WHAT HE'D BEEN up to since the summer. 'No time,' he said. 'It's what's about to happen that's our concern now.'

'Your concern,' said Hal, quickly.

Lugh laughed. 'The same Hal,' he said. 'You're quite right. It's wise not to jump straight into the unknown.'

'Never mind the unknown,' said Hal. 'I don't want to jump into *anything* to do with this world. But there doesn't seem to be much choice,' he added, aggrieved.

Lugh laughed. 'What about you, Gilly?'

'I want to find Ben, if he's in this world like us,' said Gilly firmly. 'He's not fit to be out on his own.'

'Fitter than you may think,' said Lugh. 'Ben *is* here, and he has a dangerous quest.'

'Quest? Like us and the talking head?'

'No, you did that because I asked you to. Ben's situation is different. He has to find the Dewstone; he has no choice.'

'Dewstone?' said Gilly.

'I knew it,' Hal burst out. 'I knew it, when I had that dream. Lugh, why Ben? Why pick on Ben? He doesn't have an easy time of it back home, and then to shoot him into some wild scheme in this world. He doesn't belong here, so why does he *have* to do anything? And how do you know all about it? Oh, I suppose it's all part of being a soothsayer.'

'Yes,' said Lugh. 'I knew that Ben would be coming, and of course I knew as soon as he came through the mist.'

'Fog.'

'Fog, then.'

'Why him?' Hal persisted. 'Go on, stop being so mysterious and tell us.'

'There are reasons,' was all that Lugh would say.

Hal looked far from convinced, and Gilly, recognising that rebellious look, cut in. 'Tell us about the Dewstone, Lugh.'

'It's an ancient stone. Small, and not very significant looking. It was made with magic, and it has magical powers. Very great powers.'

'Whose is it? And where is it?'

'It is in the keeping of its guardians,' was Lugh's unhelpful answer. 'It has power and it gives power to whoever possesses it.'

'You mean to Ben, if he finds it?'

'Possibly. There is a problem, though, because he landed up in a barn belonging to two Numens and ate an apple.'

'Numens?' asked Hal.

'Ag and Pag,' said Jouri, shaking his head. 'A nasty pair.'

'They realized that Ben might be the red-haired boy who was destined to come from another world and find the Dewstone. So they made him eat one of their apples, and now he's bound to them until he completes the task they've set him.'

'So they've sent him off to get the Dewstone,' said Jouri. 'But if he succeeds, he has to give it to them?'

'Maybe.'

'Wild Magic,' said Jouri. 'I don't like it.'

'Nor do I,' said Lugh. 'Very dangerous.'

'Wild Magic?' asked Hal.

'That's the magic of the Old Kings,' Lugh explained.

'The ones who used to rule Vemoria?'

'Yes. And if the Numens have the Dewstone, they can use it to bring the Old Kings back to Vemoria.'

'Isn't that good?' asked Gilly. 'Vemoria is an awful place.'

'The Twelve who rule Vemoria are rigid and authoritarian and oppressive, it's true. But, believe me, many Vemorians would prefer that to the terrors of the Wild Magic.'

'So it's better if Ben doesn't get the Dewstone?'

'Not better for him,' said Jouri

'No, not better for him,' said Lugh. 'And it isn't only the Numens who want the Dewstone. Others, Vemorians, would like to get their hands on it.'

'The Old Kings again?' asked Gilly.

Lugh shook his head. 'No. One of the Twelve. He'd like to oust the other eleven, and rule alone. Unpleasantly.'

'And I bet I know which one of them it is,' exclaimed Hal. 'The one with Erica.'

'Uthar, the First of the Twelve,' said Jouri. 'Dear, oh dear. That wouldn't be good for Tuan.'

'It wouldn't be good for anyone,' said Lugh.

'Does this Ben know anything about the Dewstone?' asked Jouri.

'Practically nothing, only what the Numens have chosen to tell him.'

'So, if he finds the Dewstone, he'll happily hand it over as instructed?'

'Possibly,' said Lugh.

'Then we need to find him, and warn him,' said Jouri. 'Before he gives it to those wicked witchy women, and we have to stand back and watch all hell break loose.'

'Imaginatively put.'

'How can you find him?' said Hal. 'Needle in a haystack has nothing on it. He could be anywhere.'

'No,' said Jouri, thinking hard. 'We know he's in the Thirdlands.'

'I can't go into the Thirdlands,' said Lugh. 'No soothsayers allowed. Especially not from Tuan.'

'Aha,' said Jouri.

'So you want us to go,' said Hal. 'You want us to find him.'

'I think you can.'

'We'll find him,' said Gilly.

'We don't have much choice,' said Hal glumly.

Of the Twelve who ruled Vemoria, Uthar was the tallest, darkest and most malevolent. Others were afraid of him; he was afraid of no one and nothing. That day, he sat in the Great Chamber in his palace in Galat, the capital of Vemoria, plotting with his counsellor Culun and his daughter Erica.

Culun didn't look like a counsellor. He looked plump and good-natured. It was only when you took a second look at the hard, calculating eyes buried in the little mounds of fat around his eyelids that you believed he was what he was. Head of police, chief of spies, and Uthar's right-hand man.

Erica didn't like him or trust him. Erica, half Vemorian, half Otherworlder, didn't approve of fat, unfit people. She didn't worry about Culun's treatment of his enemies and of traitors; that was his job. But she didn't think that he treated either her father or her with enough respect.

Uthar was the First of the Twelve, but that only meant that he lived in the Palace of the First, and was spokesman for the Twelve. He had no more power than the other eleven, and he knew better than to try and seize it. The last one of the Twelve rulers of Vemoria who tried that had lost his head. Literally, and it had been hung up on the highest bridge in Galat, as an example to anyone else who might stray from their allotted role in society.

Culun stepped forward and handed Uthar some papers. Uthar's thin mouth twitched from time to time as his sharp mind absorbed and recorded the information he was reading.

Erica was longing to know what was in the papers, but she wasn't going to ask her father in front of Culun.

He glanced up, saw her expression, laughed his cold laugh, and told her. 'Culun's spy in the quarries on our boundaries with the Gonelands has sent a report. Two strangers appeared there.'

'Sent to the quarries?'

'No, creeping around in the tunnels. He says,' and Uthar flipped over the page, 'he says that they were intruders. Otherworlders, he's almost sure.'

'He's arrested them, is bringing them in for questioning?'

'Unfortunately not,' said Culun smoothly. 'He had alerted the guards, but there was a rockfall, and they disappeared.'

'They could be buried under the rocks,' said Uthar with a frown, 'Or they could have escaped.'

'Unlikely,' said Culun. 'If they did, they won't have got far, there was a terrible blizzard across those mountains that night.'

'What were they like?' Erica asked.

'Young,' said Culun. 'Older boy, younger girl.'

Uthar and Erica looked at each other. 'They must have come through,' said Uthar flatly.

'I wonder why,' said Erica.

Culun put two and two together. 'These are the two who were here before, in that business of the head.'

'Yes,' said Erica.

'And you went to see them? In the Otherworld.'

'There is now a way through, from where they live,' said Uthar grimly. 'And there have been these rumours about the boy with red hair, an Otherworlder, coming through to find the Dewstone.'

Culun nodded. 'I have heard this.'

'We wanted to ask some question, to find out if there was such a boy living nearby, visiting, perhaps ...'

'And they told you?'

'We found a tree of the Old Kings blossoming and bearing apples in their garden. An absurd sight, in a pathetic patch of suburban scrub. It was foggy; their not very intelligent mother was there, but they were nowhere to be seen.'

Culun knew what the apple tree meant. 'Disgraceful,' he said. 'That could leave openings for a large area all around. Who knows who may have come through?'

'Who indeed,' said Uthar. He thought for a few dark moments. 'Culun,' he said, raising his head. 'Is there any news in from the Land of the Gods? Because if someone else came through, then that's where they might have gone.'

'One or two whispers of some strange goings-on have reached me,' Culun admitted.

'Then why is there no report?'

'Of rumours? Unsubstantiated rumours? If I passed all those on, you'd have no time for anything else. I need to sift, and appraise, and check my sources. As I am now doing on this matter.'

'As soon as you hear anything, you let me know.'

Culun's lip curled. 'Naturally.'

Uthar wasn't letting him off the hook. 'Where do you expect more information to come from?'

'I believe,' said Culun reluctantly, 'I believe, and there is no evidence yet, that the Numens Ag and Pag are involved in some piece of mischief to do with this.'

'That appalling pair,' said Uthar. He turned to Erica. 'You wouldn't like them at all. Horrible old hags.'

'I look forward to meeting them,' said Erica evilly.

Eleven

*A*G AND PAG HAD MADE THEMSELVES A CELEBRA-tory meal, a disgusting mess of bad fish and greasy bones.

'Delicious,' said Ag, wiping her oily chin with the back of her hand. 'Pass the jug.'

Both Ag and Pag had taken too many swigs from the jug already, but they were too pleased with themselves and with life to notice. Or to notice the figure who had slipped noiselessly into the barn through the partly open door.

'Too dangerous,' Culun's snout had been warned by a fellow spy. 'Those Numens will eat you alive.'

'They've got to catch me first,' said the snout. 'And I must find out what they're up to. In the City they say that they have control of the red-headed boy, the one who can find the Dewstone.'

'Rubbish,' scoffed his friend. 'There are always rumours about a red-haired boy and the Dewstone. That Dewstone disappeared so long ago that not even the demigods know where it is. No one has ever seen it, and so no one can find it. This prophecy about a child with red hair coming to the Thirdlands and claiming the Dewstone is a nurse's story, told to frighten Vemorian children in their beds.'

'If it were true … And there have been signs.'

'Signs! If you want to waste time on signs, go ahead. I

wouldn't. And I certainly wouldn't risk trying to tiptoe round the Numens' den. Foolhardy, I call it.'

'Orders from Culun.'

'In that case ...' He shrugged.

'I'll be in Culun's good books when I bring back news of the Dewstone.'

'The Twelve aren't interested in fairy tales.'

No, thought the snout. But don't tell me that Uthar won't be seriously interested in the Dewstone; all that power. He kept his thoughts to himself.

'You've got this fixed idea about the Dewstone, so carry on. Go and snoop on Ag and Pag, if you dare. Just don't expect me to rescue you.'

'I shan't need rescuing,' he said with a knowing smile. 'Those Numens have been celebrating, and celebrating hard, from what I hear. They think the Dewstone is as good as in their hands, for them to make dreadful mischief with. They'll have been downing the *roisin*; a few jugs of that and they wouldn't notice if the Lord of the Dragons himself came whizzing down the chimney.'

He was right. By the time he arrived, Ag and Pag were in an advanced state of merriment, and were crowing about what they were going to do.

'With the Dewstone,' said Ag extravagantly, 'We can do what we like.'

'War in the Gonelands,' said Pag with satisfaction. 'Rebellion in Tuan. Magic in Vemoria. Lots and lots of magic, and the Old Kings ruling again, ruling with wild magic.'

'Goody,' said Ag, with a loud hiccup.

'Tee hee,' said Pag. 'Even give some of the demigods a bit of a shock; they all despise Numens ... but we'll show them.'

Ag collapsed to the ground in a fit of raucous mirth, rolling about and kicking her feet in the air. 'They think it's a story, that the Dewstone's gone from history. Let them wait. The Red One's come, and he's in our power, and we will have it.'

Pag gave another heaving burp, and pulled Ag up off the floor. 'Will the boy get into the Tower of Troubles? And, if he does, will he find the map?'

'He will, he will! Because he *is* the Red One, and his hand will fit the print and he will get into the Tower of Troubles, and find the map; oh, I'm sure of it.'

The snout crept silently out.

Unnoticed.

Ben had been so tired that he had barely noticed his surroundings the night before, when he had sunk into the sleep of exhaustion.

Now, as light streamed in through the window, he uncurled himself, wondering for a few seconds where he was, before he remembered. He was in the City of Towers. He stretched and looked around. He was lying on a thin mattress, with the Dollop stretched out beside him, paws relaxed, big grey eyes closed. He put out a hand and gave his fur a stroke. It was silky and warm, and a gentle rumble began in the great cat's throat. His tail flicked, his paws flexed, showing huge claws, and as he opened his eyes, he gave a great and fishy yawn.

'Even the pads of your paws are grey,' Ben told him. Funny, he had never taken much notice of cats, but he was really glad to wake up and find the Dollop there. But where was Tarquin? He and the Dollop were alone in the small round stone room, high above the street.

Then he remembered, as a vague picture of a flying dragon floated into his mind. Not just a dragon, in fact, but several dragons. Circling in the sky, then floating down on their scaly wings, then soaring again with a single flap ... and that little dragon, was that Tarquin?

Then those other dragons must be huge, thought Ben with awe. And where was the picture coming from? The Dollop, no doubt.

The image of the dragons faded, to be replaced by a heap of fish. The Dollop, Ben gathered, was hungry.

'It's all very well,' he said, clattering down the stone spiral staircase behind the Dollop, 'but I can't eat raw fish for breakfast.'

'Nobody supposed you could,' said Tarquin's voice, so close that Ben jumped.

'Have you finished your dawn flight?' he asked.

'Dawn was some time ago,' said the dragon. 'Come along, come along. Or you can stay here all day if you want to, it's entirely up to you. But we dragons need food after flying, so I'm going this way.'

Ben trotted after the dragon and the Dollop, who set off down the street at a good pace. What about my breakfast? thought Ben, who was feeling very hungry. Then his attention was distracted by the Dollop, who stopped, swished his tail, and dabbed a paw at what looked like a small heap of rubbish at the side of the street.

The dragon looked round to see why they had stopped. 'Ah,' he said. 'The Dollop's found something. Have a look, see what it is.'

'In that rubbish?'

'Dollop's have an instinct for some things,' said the dragon, swooshing aside the rest of the rubbish with a contemptuous claw. 'There you are, told you so.'

Ben leant over to see what the dragon was talking about, and there, in the gutter was a shiny gold coin.

'Pick it up,' said Tarquin. 'Then we can be on our way.'

'But it must be valuable,' said Ben. 'Shouldn't I find out whose it is?'

'You never would,' said the dragon practically. 'It's been thrown away. If you leave it, the next person coming along will pick it up. Or the rubbish collector, and he's so rich with his pickings over the years that he certainly doesn't need it.'

'If you say so,' said Ben, picking up the heavy coin. 'How much is it worth?'

'Enough to buy you several meals,' said Tarquin.

'And fish for you and the Dollop?'

The dragon's scales showed a pleased blue and gold colour for a brief minute before turning back to the yellow and green scales of the hungry dragon. 'That's a kind thought, boy,' he said. 'But the Dollop and I have no need to buy our food.' He sniffed, curling up his big nostrils. 'I think I can smell bread.'

He could, and as they turned the corner, Ben could see a shop doing a brisk early morning business in bread rolls. The shopkeeper bit the gold coin suspiciously, and then handed over two fresh rolls cut and smothered with honey, together with a handful of change.

'Check it,' said Tarquin. 'Huh, just as I thought. Shopkeeper, check your sums.'

The shopkeeper wasn't at all abashed, but he gave the dragon a sour grin, and changed some of the coins in Ben's outstretched palm.

'That's better,' said Tarquin. 'Now, this way. We're off to the lake.'

Ben sat on a large, flat, warm stone by the side of the big lake that stretched alongside part of the City of Towers. He was quite happy, sitting there in the sun, eating his rolls and watching the dragon and the Dollop fishing. They had very different techniques. The Dollop sat at the water's edge, utterly still, concentrating intently.

Then a huge paw shot out and scooped a gleaming silver fish on to the shore.

Meanwhile Tarquin skimmed to and fro over the surface of the still water, like a huge bird, then hovered and plunged head first into the lake to emerge with a similar fish in his strong jaws. You could see where he had dived, as he left a little area of steam behind him each time.

'That's better,' said Tarquin, swallowing the last of his catch with a dragonsize burp. He licked his chops with his long tongue, and looked at the Dollop, who was busy washing his whiskers. 'Don't get started on that, or we'll be here all morning,' he said. 'It takes Dollops hours once they start washing,' he explained to Ben as they moved off along the shore.

'Don't they need to do it?'

'Time enough for that later,' said the dragon.

The lake sparkled and glimmered in the slanting sunlight. It was slightly misty, and the water and the sky merged in a pale, pinky-purple haze. Screwing his eyes up, Ben could just make out the far side of the lake.

'Are those buildings?' he asked, shading his eyes with his hand.

'Over there? That's the part where the gods live,' said Tarquin, marching along with his tail making swirling patterns on the shingle.

'Gods?' said Ben, struggling to keep up.

'Gods,' said Tarquin. 'Demigods and Immortals this side of the lake, together with all the other riff-raff. The top lot live over there. Do themselves very well, I believe. Of course, we dragons don't take much notice. Plenty of dragons around before that crowd moved in.'

'How can they be gods?'

'Same as anywhere else,' said Tarquin indifferently. 'Don't die, although they can end up in strange places.

Certain powers, easy lifestyle, and they like playing about with other people's lives. Oh, and they're all related, and they all quarrel a lot. Some of them go out and do great deeds, but mostly they keep themselves to themselves. Best thing, really, you wouldn't want that lot out and about.'

'A message? From the Thirdlands?'

The guard bowed.

Erica, at her father's side, said nothing.

'A message for the Council of the Twelve,' said the guard.

'Give it to me.'

The guard hesitated.

'I am First of the Twelve. You may give it to me. I will call the Twelve together. Go, you've done your duty. And send Culun to me.'

'He's seen the message,' said the guard.

'Has he indeed?' said Uthar, not looking up.

The guard bowed, turned on his heel and left. 'Phew,' he said, once out of earshot. 'Gives me the creeps, that one. And the girl. She's just as bad.'

Another guard sniffed in agreement. 'Took the message, did he?'

'Yes.'

'That's the last anyone will see of it.'

'See of what?' said a senior guard, materialising from nowhere.

'My buckle,' said the first guard, improvising rapidly. 'It fell off ... into ... into a canal.'

'You will be fined for carelessness. I hope there was nothing more to your whispered conversation. Treason against the State is a grave offence.'

He went on his way.

'As if we didn't know,' said the second guard, bitterly.

Twelve

CULUN CAME IN AS UTHAR WAS READING THE message, with Erica looking over his shoulder. They were in the marbled council chamber, and his footsteps echoed as he walked over to the pair of them and bowed to Uthar.

Uthar handed the message to Culun. 'Burn it.'

'Is your spy still there?' Erica asked.

'Yes,' said Culun.

'Where?' asked Uthar.

'He's back in the City of Towers. Listening. Following up leads.'

'That's his job.' Uthar stroked his chin. 'The Red One. And the Dewstone. It's an old story.'

'Maybe that's all it is. A story.'

'Maybe, maybe not,' said Uthar.

'I suppose plenty of strange things go on in the Land of the Gods,' said Culun, 'and we all know there was a Dewstone once.'

'Yes, but it vanished generations ago,' pointed out Erica.

Culun was following his own line of thought. 'All that stuff about a boy with red hair coming from another time and another place and journeying over the water to the Tower of Troubles ... it sounds very unlikely. And no one ever has seen the Tower of Troubles, that only exists in legend as far as one knows.' He shook his head doubtfully.

'I suppose,' said Uthar, 'that if the story's true ...'

'A big if,' said Erica.

'Then there will be something in the Tower to tell the boy where to find the Dewstone.'

'No one who had the Dewstone would ever give it up willingly,' said Culun. 'So even if he knows where it is, it doesn't mean he can get his hands on it.'

'Depends where it is and who's got it. Perhaps whoever has it, or whatever has it, has to give it up when this particular boy asks for it.'

'Hooey,' said Erica. 'If there's such a thing as this Dewstone, then I agree with Culun. No one would give it up.'

Uthar flashed a sinister smile.

'On the other hand, who would want to put a young boy in danger? Surely, if he leads us to the place where the Dewstone is, why, we can claim it for him. Save him the trouble.'

'Even though you aren't the chosen one?' said Culun.

Uthar gave a sardonic laugh. 'There's giving and there's taking, Culun. I don't need to tell you that.'

'The legend says the Dewstone has magical powers.'

'Magic is treason in Vemoria.'

'The First of the Twelve doesn't talk treason, Erica. And don't underestimate the power bestowed by the Dewstone. It could be extremely useful. I wonder ...'

Erica looked at her father in astonishment. 'You don't *believe* all this about the Dewstone and the Red One?'

Uthar was brooding, watched intently by Culun. 'These Numens ...'

'A kind of witch. Immortal, they say. Full of malice and trickery. They live by themselves, no one cares to be near them. They are dangerous when roused.'

'And full of folly,' mused Uthar. He rose, and began to pace up and down the room. 'Otherworlders in the quarries, and now the Numens boasting about the Red One. On top of what we heard before, those warnings; I don't like it.'

'Rumours,' said Erica.

'I don't pay my spies for rumours,' Uthar said bitingly.

'So what do we do?' asked Culun.

'Nothing, until we know more. Facts, Culun, that's what we want. Facts, details. Precise information. Then we can act.'

Culun walked towards the great wooden doors.

'Wait.'

He waited.

'Put out an alert. A general alert. That there might be Otherworlders in Vemoria again. Dangerous enemies of the State. To be brought here.'

'I have done so,' said Culun.

'Preferably in one piece.'

'Where are we?' asked Gilly, pausing to rub aching calves, and looking out over the endless snowy landscapes. Forest, foothills, mountains. Snow and snow and more snow.

'Just by the Spellbound Gorge,' said Jouri. 'On the boundary between the Gonelands and the Thirdlands.

'Oh, no,' said Hal, remembering their last encounter with a resident of the Thirdlands. 'I can just imagine it, full of types like the talking head, who must be at least eight foot tall, and with a nasty nature to match.'

'Quite a few of those, but Immortals and demigods and ... well, they're a mixed bunch.'

'Mixed?' Hal was suspicious. 'Sizewise?'

'All shapes and sizes,' said Jouri cheerfully. 'Different sorts, too. Some quite friendly, others best avoided.'

'And how do we know which is which?' asked Gilly.

'Mostly you don't, until it's too late.'

'And how do we get into this fascinating place?' asked Hal.

'Across a bridge. You'll see it as soon as we get through the trees.'

Gilly would rather they couldn't. She stood dismayed, looking at the curved thread of stone which soared above the dark gorge.

Hal went to the edge, ignoring Gilly's yells to him to keep back. 'It's so deep you can't see the bottom,' he remarked. And then, to Jouri, 'You'll never get Gilly to go over that,' he said.

Gilly looked across the ravine. It looked exactly the same to her on the other side: snow-covered fields, trees, an occasional group of houses. She looked across as one would in a dream, because there was no way she could cross the bridge.

'You can,' said Jouri, coming over to her. 'It's wider than it looks.'

'I don't care how much wider it is than it looks; it's still very narrow, very dangerous, and if I set foot on it, I'll be paralysed with fear. And if I dragged myself halfway across, I'd know I was going to fall, and I'd topple off ...' She shuddered. 'It makes me go cold all down my back just to think of it.'

Her voice tailed away as her eye was caught by a glowing ball hung on a thread of ribbon, which Jouri was dangling in front of her. She couldn't blink, or not look at it.

Jouri began to swing it slowly backwards and forwards.

Hal darted forward. 'You're hypnotising her. Stop it, that can be really dangerous.'

Jouri made a sharp sign to him to keep back, never faltering in the steady swing of the little jewel. 'It's necessary,' he said in a calm voice. 'Gilly must cross the bridge. This is the only way.'

'You won't succeed,' warned Hal. 'Gilly's not that kind of person, and no muttered mumbo-jumbo is going to make her cross that bridge.'

'Okay,' said Hal, ten minutes later. 'So you were right, and I was wrong.'

It had been a distinctly hairy crossing, and he rather wished that Jouri had put him in a trance. Gilly had tripped across, eyes open and unwavering, never looking up or down or left to right. There had been a terrible moment when Jouri had faltered and almost slipped, but he had regained his balance and made it to the other side.

'I thought you were going to go over then,' said Hal.

'It's a tricky business, crossing the gorge,' was all Jouri said. 'Now, time to bring Gilly out of her trance.' He paused, head on one side. 'Do you think she would like not to be afraid of heights ever again?' he asked Hal. 'I can fix that.'

Hal's first thought was that would be a very good idea. Then conscience hit him. 'I'm all for it,' he said, 'but I think she ought to say, not me. Can you do it again? Hypnotise her, I mean?'

'Possibly,' said Jouri.

'Then leave it for now.'

'Okay,' said Jouri, and began to count Gilly back to normality. She blinked several times, and shook her head. 'I can't do it, Jouri,' she began, and then looked around her. 'Where are we?'

'On the other side,' said Hal. 'Well done, Gilly, you did it.'

'I crossed that bridge?'

'You did,' said Jouri.

'I don't remember crossing it,' said Gilly, stunned.

'Look,' shouted Hal, and the other two turned back to look over the gorge.

Before their eyes, the seemingly solid stone bridge was shimmering and dissolving into thousands of spots of light. Then it was gone, leaving a pale arch of mist drifting above the gorge.

'Wow,' said Hal.

'What's happened to it?' said Gilly.

'It comes and goes,' said Jouri. 'We were meant to cross, and so it was there. None of us is meant to go back – at least, not yet – and so it's gone.'

The snow was no more than a chilly memory for Ben, as he dabbled his hands in the warm water of the lake. He was afloat in a small boat, with the Dollop, who didn't like being on the water at all, sitting huffily beside him. Tarquin had chosen to fly.

Ben's mind filled with thoughts of darkening skies, billowing waves, the boat capsizing, foamy water rushing past his ears, uncomfortable wetness ... He put out a hand and rubbed the Dollop's nose. 'Cheer up, Dollop,' he said. 'The lake's as calm as can be, and the boatman knows what he's doing.'

The Dollop's big grey eyes were watching the boatman, and he gave a deep-throated growl. The boatman looked nervously round and increased his speed. He was using a single oar to move and steer the boat, and Ben was impressed by his skill.

But if the oar's on one side, he thought, then why aren't we going round and round in circles? Then he looked down the line of the slim and high-prowed boat, and noticed that it was asymmetrical. Like the gondolas in Venice, he realized. The design of the boat allowed for the lopsided rowing. Brilliant!

They were coming nearer and nearer to the island in the centre of the lake. It was small, hardly more than a mound. There was nothing on it except for the one tall tower, which soared up to some strangely pointed battlements at the very top.

No windows, thought Ben. That must be the Tower of Troubles, he supposed. What a weird building.

As they approached, with the boatman steering the boat skilfully through the surrounding rocks, Ben could see the dragon, wings folded and tail coiled, waiting for them. He was quite blue; what's he thinking about? wondered Ben.

The Dollop leapt on to land with such force that the little boat nearly turned over. Ben was glad he'd got off first, as he jumped out of the way of the big cat.

'Come along,' said the dragon. 'We haven't got all day.'

Thirteen

'I'M OFF,' SAID THE BOATMAN, LIFTING HIS OAR TO push away from the island.

'You are not,' said Tarquin, wresting the oar from him with one swift wrench of his powerful claw. He soared into the air and then swooped down to the top of the tower, where he deposited the oar.

The boatman looked up in disbelief. 'Bring it back,' he shouted. 'That's my oar. You can't do that.'

'Don't be ridiculous,' said Tarquin, making a graceful landing. 'I just have. Now be quiet. We shouldn't be long.'

Ben had been investigating. 'Where are we?' he asked Tarquin. 'Is this the Tower of Troubles? Why isn't there a door? In fact there's no entrance of any kind.'

'That's quite usual,' said the dragon. 'In fact, I'd have been surprised if there was a door. How do you think they've kept everybody out for the last millennium if there were a door there? No, no, that's not how you get into a tower like this.'

'Is it open at the top?' Ben asked doubtfully.

'It is not.'

'Then how ...?'

The dragon pointed to where the Dollop, whiskers forward, fur up, tail low and swishing, was prowling round the base of the tower.

'Oh,' said Ben. 'It's very confusing, just grey stones,

and … How strange! For a moment I thought I saw the shape of a hand. In the stone.'

'That's what we want,' said the dragon, moving briskly round to where the Dollop was regarding a perfectly ordinary section of stonework with a fixed grey gaze.

'There's nothing there,' said Ben, disappointed.

'Concentrate,' hissed Tarquin.

Ben looked at the stone wall as hard as he could. It was no good, they were just plain, unmarked stones, each fitting exactly into the ones adjoining it. No mortar, thought Ben. How did they do that?

And at that moment, he saw, quite clearly this time, the outline of a hand.

'Put your own hand there,' said the dragon. 'Quickly, it will only last for a few seconds.'

Ben stepped forward and felt his hand drawn towards the stone as though it was magnetic. His hand fitted exactly in the fading shape, and as he made contact, there was a rumbling sound, and a whole part of the wall slid open.

Ben jumped back, nearly landing on the Dollop's paw.

'Now what?' he asked in a whisper. Directly in front of him he could see a narrow staircase, spiralling up into the tower.

'Up you go,' said the dragon.

'Not by myself,' said Ben.

He got a sudden picture of the Dollop stuck firmly between the wall and the central stone support; and as for Tarquin, he was too large a dragon to even think of going through the door.

'Alone,' said the dragon firmly.

'I can't,' said Ben. 'And where does it go?'

'To the top,' said Tarquin unhelpfully.

'And what's there?'

'According to Ag and Pag, a map to tell you where the Dewstone is.'

'Yes, but what use is a map of a country I don't know?' said Ben reasonably. 'Can I bring it down with me?'

'I really don't know,' said the dragon. 'Of course, you can try, it's entirely up to you. You just have to remember that maps come in all forms; at least magical maps do. It may be too big to move, or fade away as you look at it.'

'Oh,' said Ben.

'In which case, you'll need to memorise it.'

'So you don't know exactly what I'm looking for?'

'Um, I wouldn't say that,' said the dragon. 'I expect you'll know when you've found it,' he added helpfully. 'Off you go now; the door won't stay open for ever.'

Ben found himself propelled firmly forward through the door. As he put his foot on the first step, the wall slid shut behind him. Oh, no, he thought, as his heart gave an uneasy lurch. He was shut in! Maybe for ever. And there were no windows, he'd seen that from the outside. If there are no windows, said the sensible part of him, how come you can see the steps?

There must be light coming down from above, Ben decided. Then a Dollopy image wafted into his head, and he felt as though he was being given a gentle, furry shove.

Oh well, he said to himself. Here goes.

The Dollop waited at the foot of the tower, his tail just moving at its tip, his grey eyes watchful.

Tarquin was flying, circling the tower with long, gliding dives.

Far out across the lake, a fishing boat bobbed gently

on the calm surface. An apparently normal, everyday scene. But was it? The Dollop's ears went up, and the dragon made another swoop, hovered, and then flew off in a leisurely way to investigate.

A single fisherman out at this time of day was not an everyday sight, thought the dragon. What else could he be?

A spy, the dragon said to himself.

Whose spy? The dragon gave an extra swoop, giving the man in the boat a fright. Uthar's, probably. Spies were his trademark.

Uthar stood on the balcony of the house of the First Ruler and watched Erica approaching in the state boat. It drew alongside at the landing stage where the lawns sloped down to the main canal. She jumped out of the boat, without a word of thanks or farewell to the boatmen, and ran to meet her father.

'I've had more news,' he said. 'Of the Otherworlders. I think we can be sure that they are Gilly and Hal.'

Erica drew in her breath with a sharp sound. 'Where are they?'

'They've crossed the Spellbound Gorge, and are in the Thirdlands.'

'Alone?'

'Apparently not. They have some kind of a guide.'

Erica was looking particularly foxy, her face sharp and boding ill for anyone who crossed her. 'And the boy?'

Uthar rubbed his hands together. 'No news yet, but there will be. We shall certainly hear if he has found the Tower of Troubles.'

'He may reach it,' said Erica. 'Will he be able to get inside it?'

'He will, if he's the Red One.'

'I still don't believe it.'

Uthar took no notice of her scepticism.

'If, and I say *if*, this boy does find out where the Dewstone is, then he'll lead us there. And we shall see to it that *we* have the Dewstone, not those Numens, or the old kings, or anyone else. And when we have the Dewstone ...'

'We'll ... ,' Erica began.

'... use it for the benefit of the State,' Uthar interrupted smoothly.

Erica opened her mouth to say more, but a tiny gesture from her father's hand silenced her.

'We shall have news soon,' Uthar said. 'Nothing is secret in Vemoria, nor can anything be kept a secret from Vemoria's spies beyond our boundaries. Even the walls have ears.'

'You're right,' said Erica, biting her lip. 'Nothing is secret in Vemoria.'

Jouri seemed to know where he was going, because as soon as they had their skis back on, he led them off at a brisk pace. Hal caught up with him, and panted a query, but Jouri was terse. 'We need to find the Numens,' he said. 'Lugh told me where their hideout might be. Watch out for a barn, or a deserted farm building.'

They saw several, but they were all attached to prosperous-looking farms or houses; not the kind of place where the Numens would feel at home, Jouri said, dismissing them with a quick look.

When he saw the barn, though, he knew at once that it was the one. He put up a hand to stop Gilly and Hal, and then slipped down the last fifty yards alone, tense and wary. 'I don't like the look of this,' he muttered under his breath.

'What's the matter?' said Hal, surprised. 'It's just a

barn. You can see it's empty, there can't have been anyone near the place for months.'

'I think you're wrong there,' said Jouri. Then his eyes flew to a nearby tree. 'Ha,' he said. 'I felt I was being watched. Come down out of there, whoever you are.'

Gilly had to laugh as a scrap of a boy with tousled fair hair landed at their feet. 'You don't have to worry about him,' she said.

'It's not him I'm bothered about,' said Jouri. 'Now, boy, whose barn is this?'

'It belongs to the Numens,' said the boy at once. 'Horrible hags, they are. My mum says I'm not to have anything to do with them.' He dropped his voice to a macabre whisper. 'They eat children, you know.'

Jouri didn't take this as a joke, although he could see that Hal and Gilly did. 'Numens aren't funny,' Jouri said. 'I would have thought you would have remembered from your last visit how dangerous some people and places here can be.' He turned his attention back to the boy. 'If you're scared of the Numens, why are you playing so close to the barn? Are they away?'

'No,' said the boy. 'Not them. They're inside, but they drank so much *roisin*, they passed out. Snoring away like a couple of pigs, they are.'

'Do they often do that? Drink, I mean?'

'Not often. They're too mean. But they've got hold of a lad, not from here, or even from this world, my dad says. Redhead, he is, and that means something to them two. So they're celebrating.'

Hal and Gilly looked at each other.

'Where is this boy? Is he a captive?'

'Not here,' said the boy, getting restless under Jouri's staccato-fired questions. 'I don't know where he is. He's their slave, because he ate one of their apples. Stupid, we all know not to touch anything of theirs.'

'Do you know where he's gone?'

The boy shrugged. 'To find treasure for the old bags, that's what I reckon.'

'Catch,' said Jouri, throwing the boy a crystallised peach. 'Now, be off home.'

'If you're going in there,' said the boy as he skipped off, 'remember what I said, and don't eat anything.'

Hal followed Jouri into the darkness. As he pulled the door open to let more light in, they saw the heap made by the two Numens just inside the barn. Hal jumped back as though from a giant spider as Ag twisted over, mumbling in her stupor.

'Sent him to the Tower of Troubles,' she mumbled. 'Tee hee, what power, all ours, all ours ...' Her voice died away into a violent hiccup, and some more deep and disgusting snores.

'Hey, there's a horrible smell in here,' said Hal, flapping a hand in front of his nose as he beat a hasty retreat.

Jouri joined him outside, and the two of them took chill gulps of fresh air.

Gilly looked at them in surprise. 'So?'

'So, Ben isn't here.'

'Where is he, then?' said Gilly.

'We don't have any idea,' said Jouri with a warning look at Hal. 'No clues in there.'

Hal opened his mouth, saw Jouri's face and shut it again. 'No,' he said. 'They can't tell us, those Numen-whatsits. They're out for the count.'

'What now?' Gilly felt cold despair creeping over her. This was a difficult journey, full of frights. And what for? It had been easier last time, when they had a clear task to complete.

'You've got a task this time,' said Jouri.

—— 108 ——

'Yes,' said Hal. 'We have to find Ben, Gilly. We can't leave him stranded among this lot.'

'Quite right,' said Jouri. 'Now, we have to think about where we're going to go next.'

He propped himself up against a low-lying branch of a tree, and taking out a pocket knife, began to whittle away at a twig he had picked up. Hal and Gilly watched him in silence, wondering what he was up to.

'Thinking,' said Jouri. 'Hal, did you notice a door in there?'

Hal thought for a moment, trying to visualize the inside of the barn. 'Yes, there was one.'

'Open, or shut?'

'Partly open,' said Hal.

'Snow on the other side, trees and so on?'

'Now you come to mention it, no,' said Hal slowly.

Jouri casually blew the dust off the piece of wood he was working on, and smoothed it with his finger. 'So, we head for the City of Towers, do we? It's a strange place.'

'Do we have any choice?' said Hal, who felt cross with Jouri. He's playing games with us, he thought with a flash of irritation.

'No,' said Jouri. 'Not if you want to find Ben.'

'Come on,' said Hal. 'Hold your nose, Gilly.'

Fourteen

'*I* CAN'T BELIEVE THERE ARE SO MANY STEPS,' BEN said out loud.

He had started by counting them as he climbed, but he had given up at a hundred and seventy-two. They weren't shallow steps, either. And no resting places, just turn after turn of the steep stone staircase.

He paused, to rub his legs. And then I shall have to go down, he told himself. Which may be even worse, although I'll have more puff. Perhaps there's a hole at the top, and Tarquin can carry me down.

If there were a hole at the top, Tarquin could have flown up with him in the first place.

And if not a hole looking up into the blue, blue sky, then what? Ben wasn't given to alarming fancies, but he did wonder what might live in such a place.

A giant spider, huge legs dangling down to grasp him as he climbed up the final few steps?

A sorcerer, with bony hands and attendant creatures?

A mad astronomer?

A drippy girl with long blonde hair, waiting to be rescued? If so, wait on, decided Ben.

A vast, brooding eagle, with terrible golden eyes, and cruel talons?

Without noticing, Ben had reached the top of the staircase. His attention was on the horrors that might be lurking up there, and so …

Thump …

Ben took a step in mid-air, stumbled, lost his balance, grabbed the nearest thing to steady himself …

… and ended up in a heap of shelves and dust. He sat and watched as a huge pale-blue egg, just a little bigger than an ostrich egg, slowly rolled down what was left of the top shelf. It balanced for a fraction of a second and then plummeted to the stone floor. Where it bounced gently, rolled a few inches, and then came to a standstill, rocking gently.

Hard-boiled, thought Ben. Then he looked at the egg again, now lying on its side. It wasn't an egg, of course, when you looked at it properly. Not a real egg, with a shell. It was made of some stone, which was filled with light and wisps of darker colours. Ben was fascinated.

Crash.

Ben jumped, stopped gazing at the beautiful blue egg, and, for the first time, took in his surroundings as another shelf wobbled and fell.

The small round room was tiny, and suffused with a pale green light. That came from some translucent covering in the roof. A kind of greenish mother-of-pearl, thought Ben. Otherwise, now that he had brought the only furniture in the room down to the floor, the room was entirely empty.

All that effort, thought Ben indignantly. He had climbed about a thousand steps, filled with panic, and what was there to show for it? Dust, some crumbling woodwork … and, of course, the egg. Tower of Troubles; well, Ben thought to himself, that's a good name. A lot of trouble, and nothing to show for it.

He got to his feet, and gave one or two violent sneezes. Was there really nothing else here? His eyes roved over the walls again.

Hold on, was that a crack? In the wall, up near the

circle of light? Had that been there before? And there was another one, appearing before his very eyes, a jagged, widening line, travelling from the top of the wall to the bottom.

This tower, said Ben to himself, suddenly feeling quite cold, is about to collapse.

He suddenly remembered what the dragon had told him about maps coming in strange forms, especially magical maps. He hesitated only for a second, and then swept up the egg and hurled himself towards the doorway and on to the stairs. Behind him, there was a shudder and a terrible rumbling, as the room dissolved in a heap of rubble and choking dust which billowed after him in a ghastly grey cloud.

Ben heard another sharp noise. At his feet, this time. Another crack, but there, in the steps, which were beginning to break up in front of him. Ben gave a desperate, twisting leap, just reaching a step which was still intact. Then that, too, began to shake.

Ben had never moved so fast in his life. If there were a thousand steps, then Ben now held the world record for the thousand-step spiral stairway descent.

He shot out of the door and straight into the Dollop, who was sitting bolt upright, his tail lashing from side to side, growling.

Tarquin, bright yellow now for an emergency, landed beside them.

'Boat,' he said, flapping them forward with his wings and a whoosh of flames.

Ben tumbled head first into the boat, still clutching his egg, and the Dollop leapt in after him. The dragon soared up, dropped, circled, dropped again, and then glided only a few feet above the surface of the lake.

'Tower's going,' he snorted as he flew past. 'Terrible currents up there.'

The boatman, after one look at the cascade of stone bouncing and crashing down into the water, plied his oar with sudden strength. Ben, struggling to get his breath back, lifted his head just in time to see the tower finally crumble into nothingness.

There was a moment's complete silence, and then a low, reverberating roar, that seem to fill Ben's head. The island shook, and then disappeared, leaving a swirling pattern of darker water with ripples spreading out from it.

'Waves,' shouted the boatman. 'The waves! We'll be capsized.'

The ripples, instead of getting smaller and flatter, were getting bigger, and bigger, hurtling across the surface of the lake. The calm, serene water was transformed, in the space of a minute or so, into a raging wilderness of huge and overpowering waves.

The coats Jouri had lent them were impossible to wear now that they had passed into the City of Towers, and too hot and heavy to carry. Hal and Gilly were used to some of the ways of this world they had strayed into, but this abrupt change from winter to summer was startling.

'I could do with a long glass of icy water,' said Hal.

'Or an ice,' said Gilly. 'Proper ice-cream, in a double cone.'

They were in the same big square which Ben and Tarquin had passed through. Jouri looked around. 'You can drink from that fountain over there,' he said, pointing to a little shell-shaped fountain set into the wall behind the columns. Hal and Gilly were glad of the shelter under the colonnade; glad to drink the water; glad to douse hot faces in the cool trickle.

'Now what?' said Hal.

'We'll go to an inn I know,' said Jouri. 'Kept by a kinsman. We can leave the coats there, and I can try to get news of Ben.'

'Can't we go this way?' said Gilly, as Jouri headed off down a mean-looking alley. She preferred the wide, marbled streets, with their pale houses.

'No,' said Jouri.

'Why not?' Hal didn't fancy the alley at all.

'Mortals this way, demigods and so on that way.'

'Do you suppose,' Gilly whispered to Hal as they walked along the narrow pathway, 'that our friend the talking head is here somewhere?'

'Ask Jouri,' said Hal, skipping to avoid a pile of decaying rubbish. 'Jouri, what about the head? And the raven? Do they live here?'

'Probably,' said Jouri. He stopped at a dark wooden door, set back from the street. Above it hung a murky sign.

'What does it say?' said Gilly, squinting up at the board. 'Is that a hen on it?'

' "At the Sign of the Dragon" is what it says,' said Hal, after a moment's scrutiny.

'Doesn't look like a dragon to me,' said Gilly.

The door opened, and a tall figure looked out. When he saw Jouri, he gave a cry of delight, and grabbed him by the shoulders.

'Friends of mine,' said Jouri, gesturing with difficulty back to where the others were standing in the alley.

'Welcome,' said the innkeeper. 'Come in.' He hauled Jouri across the threshold. Gilly followed, and then Hal.

Something made Hal turn round as he ducked his head to go in through the low door. Two things happened. One was that he gave his head a nasty bang. The other was that he saw a man lurking in a doorway further down the street.

He rubbed his head, and called Jouri back. 'Someone was watching us go in,' he said. 'I'm sure of it.'

Jouri was beside him in an instant, his keen eyes darting up and down the street, and he shook his head. 'There's no one there now.'

Hal looked up and down the deserted street. 'He was here a minute ago,' he said, setting off to the end of the street, where he vanished from view for a minute or two before coming back at a slower pace. He made a thumbs-down sign.

'He must have gone the other way,' said Jouri.

They ran down the alley in the other direction, and came to a crossroads. Little fetid passages ran off from the main alley. They stopped, looking around them.

'He could be anywhere,' said Hal. 'We'll never find him.'

'Pity,' said Jouri. 'I'd like to have got a look at him. Never mind. At least you spotted him, Hal. It means that someone knows we're here and is keeping an eye on us.'

'Is this place like Vemoria?' asked Hal unenthusiastically, as they retraced their steps to the inn. 'All watchers and informers and police spies?'

'No, no. This is a place where people mind their own business.' said Jouri. 'All it means, if we're being watched, is that we *are* someone's business.'

The inn was better inside than they had expected from its dingy outside. It was cramped, and the heavily beamed ceilings were low, but it didn't smell or look dirty or give you the heebie-jeebies, as Gilly sensibly pointed out when Hal pulled a face.

'It's very stuffy in here,' he said.

'There's a small yard where we can sit,' said Jouri. 'Through that door there.'

Hal slid along the bench and looked up at Jouri. 'Sit down,' he said. 'Tell us why we're here.'

'We know that,' said Gilly impatiently. 'We've got to find Ben and tell him about the Dewstone. He could do all kinds of silly things if he doesn't know what it is.'

'Why *here*?' said Hal. 'Why should Ben have come here? Do you know where he is, Jouri?'

Jouri shook his head. 'This is a good base for us. I know the innkeeper, he's from Tuan, and a cousin, and I can trust him. I need to get out and ask some discreet questions, follow up any leads, find out if anyone's seen Ben, or knows what he's up to.'

'So you don't know whether he's in this city now or not?' persisted Hal.

'Hal, I don't have a clue where he is.'

Fifteen

BEN DIDN'T KNOW WHERE HE WAS, EITHER. He lay on a shore, his mind drifting. Waves lapped gently over his feet. The sand felt warm under his arms.

He coughed, and pulled himself to a sitting position, raising his hand to shield his eyes from the light. The glassy surface of the lake stretched out in front of him. He blinked. Where was he? Where were the dragon and the Dollop? And the boat?

Gradually, it came back to him, the wild wind and waters, the boat flung from wave to wave and finally sent skimming across the water on its side like a plank, flotsam from some larger vessel.

As his mind cleared and he looked around him, questions began to buzz in his head.

Where were the palaces of the gods?

Why couldn't he see the other side of the lake?

Why was the water so calm, after the great waves he had tumbled through?

And why was the water that strange pinky-grey colour? It hadn't looked like that before. Was it a lake at all? Ben stooped and dipped a finger into the water, tasted it. Thought so, he told himself. This was salt water. This was sea, not the lake. So how had he got from a lake to this strange sea shore?

And where were Tarquin and the Dollop?

Ben closed his eyes, but no reassuring fuzzy images drifted into his brain.

Nothing.

Silence.

Emptiness.

Despite the warmth of the air, Ben shivered. He had never felt so solitary as he did now, on this deserted sea shore. And it was so quiet. Not a sound to be heard.

No birds.

No wind rustling in the trees which lined the edge of the shore.

Strangest of all, no sound of water. The waves ran gently over the sand, breaking and foaming, but even when Ben leant over them, his ear cupped, the silence was unbroken.

Ben spoke out loud. 'Hello!' he shouted.

Not a sound.

Am I deaf? he wondered. Worse, was he dead? Had he drowned? He put his hand in his pocket, and pulled out the coins he had been given by the stall holder that morning.

Only that morning? It seemed days, weeks, half a lifetime ago. But the coins were reassuring. Ben felt vaguely that you didn't take coins with you into an afterlife. On the other hand, the coins didn't chink. They, too, made no noise, even as he let them fall into his other hand.

It must be water in my ears, he thought. Then he remembered something else, from before the capsize. He had been to the tower, and found an egg. The coloured egg from the tower ... Where was it?

There it was. With a soundless cry of relief, Ben saw it lying on the shore. He picked it up, cradling it in his hands.

'Well now.' Ben spoke silently to the egg, turning it

over and over. 'What do we do next? We can't stay here, because although the sun seems strangely pale, I think it might be going to get very hot.'

Ben turned in an arc, scanning the shore line in hope of inspiration. 'What do you think, egg?' he mouthed, taking a step or two along the shore.

He stopped, astonished. The egg looked as though the light had gone out of it; all the lovely translucent, swirling blues and turquoises were fading before his eyes.

In despair, Ben turned round, thinking he would hurl the egg into the sea. He couldn't bear to lose its shimmering beauty. But as he took a few steps the other way, the blues began to return to the egg.

Funny, thought Ben, taking a few experimental steps in the direction he had first taken. No, there the colours went again. Ben stopped, and considered.

The egg was clearly special, or it wouldn't have been up in that ghastly tower. Maybe it had special properties. Maybe it was a kind of compass. Or a map. The map he'd gone to find, which would lead him to the Dewstone? It could be a different kind of map from what he was used to. Since he was in a different world, no doubt the cartography would be as bizarre as so much else. And the dragon had more than hinted that the map would be strange.

In which case, since he liked looking at the wonderful floating blues in it, he might as well keep going in the direction which made the colours sing. About the only thing that *is* singing, he thought glumly as he set off, his eyes fixed on the egg.

He had been going for quite a time, walking along in a line parallel to the shore, when he noticed another strange thing.

No footprints.

He was walking in the wet sand on the edge of the sea, and yet his feet weren't leaving the slightest mark. Must be very firm sand, he said to himself doubtfully. Then he knelt down and traced the letters of his name in the sand. BEN. His finger sank into the sand, but, like his feet, left no indentation, not the slightest impression on the surface.

'This,' said Ben, standing up again, 'is very, very creepy.'

'Where are you going?' Hal asked Jouri.

Jouri paused by the door. 'I'm going to see if I can sniff out any information,' he said.

'About Ben? Can't we come too?' Gilly looked hopefully at Jouri.

He shook his head.

'Not just now. I'm more likely to have some luck if I'm on my own.'

'How long will you be?' asked Hal, who wasn't keen on the thought of hours tucked away in this cramped inn.

'Quite a while,' said Jouri. 'Possibly. The innkeeper will look after you, give you some food, beds ...'

'Can we go out?' said Hal. 'Explore a bit? There seem to be quite a lot of people going to and fro, and all of kinds of people, too. I don't think we'd be very noticeable.'

Jouri hesitated. 'Why not?' he said at last. 'Make sure you know your way back; these streets are a maze. If you get lost, ask for the inn, everyone knows it. Don't go out of this quarter, though. You could easily get scooped up if you stray where the Immortals and demigods live. Turn left when you go out of here. Then you can see the market, and beyond that is the lake, and the harbour.'

'Good,' said Hal, as Jouri closed the door behind him.

'Should we go?' said Gilly. 'What if Jouri finds out something right away, and we're not here when he comes back?'

'He seemed to think it would take him some time,' said Hal. 'And we needn't be away for long, just half an hour or so. It's stuffy and boring here, I'm going to go out alone if you won't come.'

Gilly had no intention of staying at the inn by herself, so they set off together to find the market.

Like Ben the day before, they found it a fascinating place. They had no money to buy anything, but, as Gilly pointed out, what was the use if they had. 'Can't take it back with us,' she said. 'We've had enough trouble with that seed.'

Hal hastily put down the revolving snake on a stick which had caught his eye. 'Let's go and look at the lake.'

Gilly had forgotten her qualms about being away from the inn.

'Let's,' she agreed. 'It's so hot, we could paddle.'

'Not in a harbour,' said Hal.

'There might be some beach as well,' said Gilly.

The water in the harbour was calm, with several boats bobbing gently up and down at anchor, or attached to the side of the harbour wall. But beyond the harbour, the lake showed white crests breaking above restless waves.

'Has there been a storm?' said Hal.

A fisherman on the beach alongside the harbour was inspecting his boat.

'There has,' he said. 'Waves so high, I've never seen the like of them. Crashing over the wall there, terrible. It's damaged my boat, I won't be putting out for a day or two.'

Hal and Gilly wandered along the shore, looking at

—— 121 ——

the debris thrown up by the waves. Planks, logs, bits of sail, a straw hat which had lost its crown.

'Hal,' said Gilly, stopping and looking out to the lake. 'Hal, what's that? Is it a big fish?'

Hal looked, and looked again. 'It might be a dolphin, something like that,' he said. 'It's floating on the surface and it isn't moving; I think it must be dead.'

A swell rolled towards them, lifting whatever it was and bringing it closer to the shore.

'It's an animal, Hal. Look, I think it's a huge dog. And I'm sure I saw it open its mouth.'

'Looks pretty dead to me,' said Hal. 'And it looks more like a big cat than a dog. Only I never saw a cat that big.'

'It's grey,' said Gilly. 'Is it a donkey?' She plunged into the water, ignoring Hal's shouts of alarm. The water was cold, and she had to battle to keep her feet with the buffeting sway of cross currents. 'Got it,' she said. 'Hal, come and help, please! It *is* a cat. A really huge cat.'

Between them, they brought the bedraggled, limp creature on to land. Gilly laid the head comfortably down in the shade of a rock, stroking the big cat between its ears. Tears ran down her face. 'It must have drowned,' she said sadly. 'And it's so lovely.'

The fisherman came over to see what they had brought ashore. 'Well, I'll be ... well, I never thought I'd see one of those in these parts. Why, whatever was it doing in the lake?'

'It's some kind of cat,' said Hal.

'That's a Dollop, that's what that is,' said the fisherman. 'Lovely, gentle creatures. But they live in the countryside, you don't get them around here. Rare, they are, very rare. Is it dead?'

'Yes,' said Hal, who was as upset as Gilly, but trying not to show it.

Gilly had gone very still, her mind clouding over as strange disconnected images flickered in front of her eyes.

'Gilly,' said Hal. 'Are you all right? Don't take on so over it, there's nothing you can do.'

'It isn't dead,' said Gilly urgently.

'It is,' said Hal.

'No, it isn't, I know it isn't. I can see inside my head that it's alive.'

The fisherman looked at Gilly with a thoughtful expression on his sunburned features. 'Dollops have strange powers, they say,' he said. 'Send messages through your mind, if you can understand them, which most can't. If she reckons this creature is alive, then let's see what we can do. I wouldn't like to lose a Dollop just through want of trying.'

Ben walked as though in a dream, moving through a silent landscape, where nothing stirred except the water, sleek and sluggish under a sun that seemed fixed at a single spot in the pale blue sky. The line of trees at the edge of the shore swayed in an unseen, unheard breeze, but each one seemed the same as the next. There were no breaks, no paths leading off.

And every time Ben altered his course, just to see, the egg faded and became a sludgy-brown colour.

Perhaps I'll go on like this forever, thought Ben. It was strange, he wasn't thirsty or hungry. His head didn't ache, his bare feet didn't get sore with the miles he was walking. I wonder what happened to my shoes, he thought. Must have got washed away. I'm better without them, heavy, clumpy black shoes from the Back to School rack. His aunt would be cross with him, though, for losing them … and his mother.

No, he mustn't think of his mother. Not here. Not now, when the possibility of getting back even to a strange place like the City of Towers seemed so unlikely. Let alone going back through a mist to a wet street in a normal town, and home to an ordinary house.

'It's breathing,' said Hal. 'I'm sure it took a breath.'

The fisherman had turned the big head on one side, and foamy water had bubbled out. A bad sign, Gilly had thought, but the fisherman took no notice, as he heaved and pressed on the creature's ribcage. And now, it was definite, there was a shudder under the ribs, a grunting noise.

'We've done it,' said Hal triumphantly.

'It's going to be all right,' said Gilly happily as the image in her mind which had so alarmingly come and gone, resolved itself into clear shapes of colour.

'You'll do,' said the fisherman, giving the Dollop a friendly pat. 'Let him lie here awhile, to recover. Then no doubt he'll be away.'

'I think his paw's hurt,' said Gilly, who had been admiring the Dollop's big grey paws. 'Here.'

'Cut himself,' said the fisherman, inspecting it. 'Best take care of him for a day or two, if he'll let you. I won't say anything about you finding him, otherwise you'll have a crowd round him, always keen on something new, folk around here.'

'Thank you,' said Gilly. 'You've been very kind.'

'I'll tell the wife, though,' said the fisherman. 'It isn't every day you get a Dollop rolling in on a wave.'

Gilly sat beside the resting Dollop, talking nonsense to him, and stroking his quickly-drying fur. 'We'll have to take him back to the inn,' said Gilly.

'I suppose so,' said Hal, doubtfully. 'I don't know if they'll have anywhere he can go.'

'They will,' said Gilly.

Hal pottered along the shore, looking to see what else had been washed up. A shoe. How strange. It was such an ordinary-looking shoe, just like the ones they wore at school ...

'Oh, no,' he said, crouching down to look at it. A name tape was visible, sewn to the lace inside the shoe. BEN FURSTOW it said, in small, blue capital letters.

'What is it?' said Gilly as Hal came panting up to the rock. 'Don't thunder about like that, you'll frighten the Dollop.'

'This was washed up on the shore,' said Hal.

'A shoe,' said Gilly impatiently. 'So what?'

Hal pulled the lace out to show her the name tape.

Gilly went quite pale. 'Ben Furstow!' she read 'Oh, no, it's Ben's shoe.' She stood up, shading her eyes and looking out across the empty water. 'Just the shoe,' she said. 'But what's happened to Ben? Where is he?'

Sixteen

ERICA TRAVELLED SWIFTLY, AND ALONE. HER SKIS made a gritty ssh, ssh sound as she moved expertly over the snow.

Uthar hadn't been too sure about their going separately. 'Better for you to travel with me and Culun,' he had said.

Erica disagreed. 'You're too well known. I can go where you can't because you'd be recognized.'

'We have spies to do that.'

'I'll find out more than they ever will, because I know exactly what I need to know, and why,' said Erica promptly. 'And whatever the spies find, the Council will get to hear about it. Whereas what I find out is strictly for your ears only.'

Uthar liked the sound of that, but he shook his head. 'It's dangerous.'

Erica was scornful. 'Dangerous? Not really. Risky, maybe, but you have to take risks.'

Uthar looked at his daughter with chilly admiration. 'You'll go whatever I say.'

'Yes,' said Erica.

'We'll meet in the City of Towers,' he said. 'How will you find your way in?'

'How will you?' said Erica.

Uthar laughed. 'I often come and go. It's not a problem.'

'Someone will show me an entrance,' said Erica confidently.

'There's a lot of magic there, don't forget that.'

'Magic holds no fears for me,' said Erica. 'A little pressure applied in the right place, and you can get what you want, magic or no magic.' She got up from the heavy, velvet-topped bench on which she had been sitting. 'See you soon, Father.'

'When we come back here,' said Uthar broodingly, 'it will be with the Dewstone in our hands.'

'And then we can deal with Hal and Gilly and the boy,' said Erica in a very nasty way. 'I've had enough of them sliding through from their world, as though they had the right ... Well, they won't be coming again. Not ever.'

Erica didn't cross into the Thirdlands by the stone bridge over the Spellbound Gorge. She knew its shifting nature and so had travelled by an old, winding route which took longer, but was more reliable. She knew she had crossed into the Thirdlands as the air became clearer and the sky a more brilliant blue. Then she looked around her for signs of life.

'Hey, pussy cat,' she called invitingly, seeing a huge grey cat hunched on a branch of a great spreading tree. 'I've got some food you'd like.'

She drew something from the pack on her back and threw it down on the ground. She waited, certain that the animal would jump down. A few twists of its tail, two or three whiskers wrenched out, and the cat would show her where there was an entrance to the City of Towers. It would know; all these animals knew that kind of thing.

Unfortunately for her, the grey creature was no pussy cat but a Dollop. Limited its brain cells might be, but it knew a trap when it saw one. Especially when it was a trap laid by someone with such dark and horrible thoughts oozing out of her mind.

The Dollop snarled, hackles rising. Then, with a great spring, it leapt into an adjoining tree and then to another. A flash of grey, and it was gone; Erica wasn't going to get any help there.

She shrugged philosophically. Win some, lose some, she told herself, although she never liked losing anything. Erica was firmly on the winning side of life. It crossed her mind for a moment that the big grey thing might pass a message on, warning others that she was here. Then she dismissed the idea as foolishness. How could it?

The boy who had helped Jouri and the others proved more amenable to reason. Holding his agonisingly painful arm, he was more than ready to direct Erica to the barn. 'And I hope them old hags eat her alive,' he said to himself, as he went yelping home to his mother.

Ag and Pag were stirring, but not really in the land of the living. They noticed a dim shadow passing through, smelt unfamiliar flesh, stirred themselves for a brief moment as the warm air from the City entrance wafted into the icy barn, and then relapsed into their noisy slumbers.

Erica had made it into the City of Towers. Now, she said to herself, all I have to do is find Hal and Gilly. Because they will be looking for this red-haired boy, the creeps, and they'll lead me to him.

Culun had arrived in the City before Erica. He was in the mortals' quarter, in an anonymous old house that he often used. He sat on an old oak chair in a gloomy room, talking about Gilly and Hal to a bony woman with a sour face. This house was a Vemorian refuge, a safe place in the shifting city. And its housekeeper was Culun's old nurse. Culun believed in keeping things in the family, as it were.

Anyone hearing that Culun had gone to call on his old nurse might have imagined him chatting to some kindly, motherly woman. She would be comfortable and cosy, would bustle about making Culun comfortable, would find him something nice to eat.

They would have thought wrong. She had greeted Culun without enthusiasm. 'Oh, it's you, is it? What are you doing here?'

'Business,' said Culun, as curt as the woman.

'Are you coming in?'

'Yes.'

There was no comfort here. What Culun's nurse possessed was an exceptionally cunning and sharp brain. Culun knew that if you had a thorny problem, his nurse was the one to bring it to.

'Planning to bring trouble to the Twelve, are you?' the nurse said, when Culun had told his story – or that part of it which he thought she needed to know. 'I don't hold with the Twelve, but I don't suppose what you're planning is going to do the people in Vemoria much good. But what's that to me? I'm never going back there, all those unpleasant waterways.'

'They'll go, Nurse. When Uthar rules. They'll be drained, so that nobody can move about, so that no foreigners can cross our land. So that Vemoria is once more as it was centuries ago.'

'Turning back the clock isn't so simple,' said his nurse. 'Still, it's nothing to do with me. You can do what you like. You need to find those two youngsters who've come through from the Otherworld, don't you. They'll find out where the boy and the Dewstone are, if anyone can.'

'Maybe,' said Culun.

'Otherworlders,' mused the nurse. She became brisk. 'Well, I never heard of any of them coming through except for a purpose, and it sounds to me as though that purpose may be to do with the other boy. The redhead. Mind you, it's an old story, and I wonder if there's any truth in it. Still, I can see that from your point of view, it's worth a try. If it works, and you can get hold of that Dewstone; well, that's the Twelve dealt with.'

'Exactly,' said Culun.

'You know where they are?'

'No.'

'Are they alone?'

'I think they're travelling with a Gonelander. A man called Jouri. He doesn't trust me.'

'Jouri? He doesn't trust his own grandmother. And who with any sense does trust you?' she added brutally. She thought for a moment. 'Leave it with me, I'll see what rumours I can pick up in the market.'

Hal and Gilly carried the Dollop back to the inn, wrapped in an old sail which the fisherman had provided. 'He can't walk, not with that hurt foot,' he had said. 'And it's best if the whole quarter doesn't see you walking along with a Dollop.'

They had to tell the innkeeper what was in the sail, and he looked on, fascinated, as they unrolled the big cat. The Dollop looked up with his great grey eyes, and the astonished innkeeper took a step back. 'My word,' he said. 'You've got something there. I've never been that close to one. Too many teeth and claws for my liking.'

The Dollop flattened his ears at him, and the innkeeper backed away.

'Don't worry,' said Hal. 'He doesn't mean it.'

A big pink tongue came out, and the Dollop, still too weak to stand, wiped it round his mouth.

'I think he's hungry,' said Gilly.

'I've got some scraps of fish,' said the innkeeper. 'He'll like those, maybe.'

The Dollop did, and by the time Jouri came back, tired and worried after a fruitless day, he found the Dollop making a feeble attempt to wash himself.

Gilly and Hal launched into a garbled account of their visit to the lake, interrupting and contradicting each other so that Jouri was thoroughly confused.

'Shut up, Hal,' said Gilly, noticing Jouri's worried face. 'Did you have any luck?'

Jouri shook his head. 'Not a whisper about Ben. Tales of a storm and a tower falling down, but what could that have to do with him?'

'We found something,' said Hal, pulling out Ben's shoe which he'd hidden under a cushion. 'Look, Ben's shoe.'

Jouri took it from him, and turned it over in his hands. 'You're sure?'

'Yes. We found it on the shore of the lake, with the Dollop,' said Gilly.

'And what was a Dollop doing there, I'd like to know,' said the innkeeper as he came briskly in with food for Jouri. 'They don't often come into the City of Towers.'

'It could have been after food,' suggested Hal. 'From the lake. Fishing. Big cats catch fish in lakes. It could have been swept away by the storm.'

'They do fish in lakes,' agreed the innkeeper. 'And in rivers, too, where they come from. But lake or no lake, that Dollop must have had a very good reason for being here. Of course, they say that they keep in touch with each other across the air. Messages on the ether. And some people can pick up what they're thinking, too.'

Hal and Gilly exchanged glances, but said nothing until the innkeeper had left the room.

'Jouri,' said Gilly urgently, shifting her foot from under her and rubbing it. 'I can see what's in the Dollop's mind. More or less.'

'Can you, now,' said Jouri. 'Ever experienced that before? Or known things were about to happen? Felt that someone you know well, like Hal, was in trouble or ill?'

'Like twins, you mean?' said Hal, interested.

Gilly shook her head. 'Never. If you'd asked me, I would have said it was impossible. But I keep on getting, well, kind of pictures, from the Dollop here. They fade away, I think he's asleep a lot. And then they come back.'

'Interesting pictures?' asked Jouri casually.

Gilly hesitated, then plunged in. 'I think the Dollop's been with Ben. Most of the time he's been here. And that something terrible happened out there, in the lake. And now the Dollop has lost contact with Ben. There are no messages or thoughts coming through from Ben, I can feel it, because I can feel that the Dollop's trying hard to make contact with him. But there's nothing from Ben, nothing at all.'

Seventeen

*A*G AND PAG WOKE UP SLOWLY IN THEIR BARN, both of them in a very bad mood.

'Horrible day,' muttered Ag, dragging herself to look out of the barn door.

'No *roisin* left,' said Pag sourly, kicking the empty jar across the barn with a plump foot.

Then they remembered, and their mood improved.

'The boy!' said Ag.

'The horrid little redhead.'

'Let's see how he's getting on,' said Ag, groping round her neck for the silver eye which hung there on a tarnished chain.

Shock!

'No chain!' wailed Ag.

Pag had made the same discovery. 'No eye,' she said grimly.

They hurled themselves on to their hands and knees, scrabbling desperately among the dust and straw and decayed apple cores on the barn floor.

'No good,' said Pag dusting down her hands as she sat back on her heels. 'They've gone.'

'They can't have gone,' cried Ag.

'When I say gone, I don't mean they left of their own accord,' said Pag. 'I mean that someone's been in and taken them. While we were resting.'

'Who would dare?' said Ag.

'No one from these parts,' said Pag. 'Hold on ...' She paused, her mouth tight, trying to use her fuddled brain to think clearly. 'Yes, I do remember. I woke up, only for a minute. Someone came through this barn. A girl. A Vemorian, I could smell her. And she left by the entrance to the City.'

'A mortal? Just walked through and into the City of Towers?' Ag was flabbergasted. 'I never heard of such a thing.'

'She didn't just walk through,' said Pag. 'She stopped long enough to steal our silver eyes from round our necks.'

'Come on,' said Ag. 'City of Towers, eh? Let's get her.'

Hal and Gilly and Jouri sat rather glumly in the inn parlour. Jouri's thoughts were elsewhere, and when Gilly asked a question, he mumbled a vague answer.

'He's not listening,' said Hal

Then Jouri suddenly came to life. 'I've had a thought,' he said, rummaging in his pocket. He drew out what looked like a pair of coins.

Gilly and Hal watched as he spat on them and gave them a rub before holding them up to the light.

'They aren't coins,' said Gilly. 'What are they, Jouri? Some kind of ornament?'

'I think they're more than that,' said Jouri. He held one up to his face and squinted through the hole in the centre.

'It's an eye,' said Hal. 'A silver eye. Where did you get them, Jouri?'

'I stole them,' said Jouri with great satisfaction. 'From the Numens, when we were in the barn. I had a feeling they might come in useful. Every Numen has one of these. They are the most precious things they possess. They use them for far-seeing.'

'Far-seeing?' Hal was sceptical.

'Do they work?' said Gilly. 'For anyone?'

'Not for me,' said Jouri. 'I just see through them, same as I would any other piece of silver with a hole in the middle.'

'You've tried, then,' said Hal, stretching out his hand to pick one up. He held it to his eye and squinted through it. 'All I can see is the wall and the tip of the Dollop's tail.'

'Let Gilly try,' said Jouri.

'Okay,' said Hal, handing her the pair of silver eyes and turning his attention back to the Dollop. The innkeeper had bound his paw up with some salve, and he was licking uneasily at the bandage.

'Hey, don't do that,' said Hal. He knelt down in front of the Dollop and stroked his head. 'You've got to leave it alone, or your paw won't heal.'

Hal wasn't watching Gilly, and he didn't notice the expression on her face as she held up first one silver eye and then the other one to her face.

'What can you see?' said Jouri softly.

A deep growl began to grow in the Dollop's throat, and the tip of his tail moved from side to side.

'Calm down, mog,' said Hal.

'It's Ben,' said Gilly, in a surprised voice. 'He's walking along by water ... It's very strange. It's a very strange place, such weird colours. And I can't hear anything ... He's lonely, I can see that he's utterly alone. Just walking ... And he's carrying something.'

'What, Gilly?' said Jouri. Hal opened his mouth to speak, but Jouri put out a restraining hand. 'What's he carrying?'

—— 135 ——

'A big blue egg. It's very beautiful. He's watching it, all the time.'

'Does he know where he is?'

'I don't think so.' Gilly turned and looked at the Dollop, whipping the silver eyes away from her own eyes. 'The Dollop knows. He can see it.'

'Look at him,' said Hal.

The Dollop had tensed every muscle, and the fur along his back and up his tail was standing on end.

'Look through the eyes again,' said Jouri urgently.

'Oh, my goodness,' said Gilly. 'I don't believe it.'

'What?' said Hal. 'Let me look.'

'It's no good,' said Jouri. 'We can't see anything through those eyes. Gilly can. Leave her be.'

'It's a huge flying creature. It's come swooping out of the sky ... it's going to attack Ben. Oh, we must stop it!'

'Gilly, are you making this up? Jouri, how can she possibly be seeing what's happening?'

'I don't know how,' said Jouri. 'But she can. I assure you, she can.'

'It's landed,' said Gilly. 'And Ben's running towards it, jumping and waving his arms. Don't, Ben, it's much bigger than you, and those talons ...'

There was silence as they all held their breath.

'It's a dragon,' said Gilly in an incredulous whisper.

Jouri's merry smile flashed out; the first time today, thought Hal.

'A dragon?' said Jouri. 'Did you say a *dragon*? What kind of dragon?'

'Just a dragon,' said Gilly impatiently.

'Big?'

Gilly's eyes never wavered as she stared through the silver holes. 'How big is big? I never saw a dragon before. Ben's smiling,' she went on. 'He isn't frightened at all. He's trying to hug it, and they're dancing round.

—— 136 ——

He's dropped the egg, and the dragon's picked it up. Now he's thrown it in the air and he's catching it. He's playing!'

The Dollop opened his mouth and let out a large roar, which subsided into great rumbling purrs. Gilly took the eyes off again and looked at the Dollop. 'You know who that is, don't you? I can see the dragon now, in my mind, and that's coming from you. I can see what's in your mind, and when I look through the silver eyes, you can see what I do.'

'This is crazy,' said Hal. 'Why Gilly? And where is Ben?'

'I think Gilly can see because I hypnotized her to get her across the bridge. Do you remember? That must have opened a channel in her mind. It's not surprising, really, when you consider where we were.'

Hal was indignant. 'Opened a channel? You turned her into some kind of a zombie?'

'Not at all,' said Jouri, who was beaming with delight. 'It's done her no harm, has it, Gilly?'

Gilly shook her head.

'No.'

'And it means we have an idea where Ben is.'

'Which is where, precisely?'

'I think he's slipped out of this world,' said Jouri. 'And out of this time. I think he's passed into the Place Between.'

'The place between what?'

'It's just the Place Between. It's out of time, and out of sound, and it's where the dragons fly.'

'Dragons,' said Hal. 'Dragons!'

'Hal,' said Gilly warningly. 'Just think of the talking head! A giant's head, which went on talking after it had been cut off? Yakked its way across two countries? And its friend, the raven. I mean, whoever saw a raven that size, let alone one that could talk as well.'

'I grant you the talking head,' said Hal irritably. 'And the nagging raven.'

'So how come you can believe that, but not dragons?'

'Because I saw them, and I haven't seen any dragons, except in books.'

'I expect you believe in lots of things you've never seen,' said Jouri.

'Such as?'

'Black holes,' said Gilly at once. 'And all sorts of other stars and things nobody's ever seen.'

Hal flushed. 'That's different. And besides ... Oh, bother the dragons. What we need to do is find Ben, and if what you're seeing is what's happening, then we haven't a hope.'

'No point in arguing,' said Jouri. 'When we meet up with Ben, then it's quite likely Hal will see a dragon for himself. Ben's obviously made a friend there.'

'When?' said Hal. 'If, the way things are going!'

'Ben, out there, with a dragon,' said Gilly. 'I do hope he's all right.'

'He has a task,' said Jouri. 'Doubtless that egg's got something to do with it. You buried the head, why shouldn't Ben do whatever it is that he has to do?'

Ag and Pag flitted angrily through the dimmest and dreariest places of the City of Towers. They had no wish to join the other Immortals in their pretty houses or walk along their broad streets. The Numens were outsiders, troublemakers, dwellers on the dark side.

'Drat it,' said Ag.

'What's up?' said Pag.

'Got a whiff, a whiff of Vemorian. Lost it.'

'Go back, sniff about,' said Pag. Ag's nose was much

better than hers, she had to admit it. But she was doubtful. 'Are you sure?'

Ag retraced her steps, snuffling the air like some decrepit hound. 'This way,' she said, flapping with a bony arm. 'It's up here. Very strong now.' She stopped abruptly. 'Well, well, well,' she said, an evil smile spreading over her unpleasant features. 'Do you know what we've got here?'

'What?'

'Wouldn't you like to know?'

Pag took a threatening step towards Ag. 'Spit it out.'

'All right, I was going to tell you.' She cackled. 'It's Uthar. Himself. Here in the City, somewhere near here.'

Pag was stunned. 'Oh, rubbish. The *roisin's* addled your wits. What would Uthar be doing here? The Twelve aren't welcome here, the demis and the Immortals don't like them at all.'

'He's here on personal business,' said Ag gleefully. 'Now, isn't that interesting?'

'He's after the Dewstone,' said Pag crossly.

'He can't have it. It's going to be ours.'

'Not if we don't find that Vemorian girl and get our eyes back. The red one will be off with the Dewstone soon as he gets his hands on it, he won't bring it back to us unless we make him. And how can we, if we can't follow him with our eyes?'

'That,' said Ag, 'is where Uthar can help us.'

It was quite different now that Tarquin was there. They couldn't talk, because of the blanket of silence.

As though some celestial hand had flicked the volume control to zero, thought Ben. He couldn't write on the sand because his fingers left no imprint. And he didn't know if dragons could read. But they could walk side by side, and they could dance, which the dragon loved to do. Slow, stately dances, or silly cavortings in the waves, or dramatic, fiery dances with flashing eyes and lots of flame and smoke.

It made Ben laugh, but he danced, too. He didn't feel lonely any more, and despite appearances, this wasn't such a desolate place. Not with Tarquin feeling so happy here.

The dragon seemed to know all about the egg. He held it up from time to time, and breathed hotly on to its gleaming surface. Ben loved that, because the colour grew more intense, and then changed into a riot of reds and purples and other blues, swirling and drifting inside the egg.

From another world, Gilly watched them. The landscape made her feel uneasy and lost, but she was glad to see Ben unafraid and with a friend. I wonder if we'll ever get to meet the dragon, she said to herself as she took off the silver eyes, and her mind came back to the mortals' quarter of the City of Towers.

I wonder if we'll ever see Ben again.

Eighteen

*E*RICA WAS HUNTING; LOOKING, SHE SAID, FOR HER cousins, visitors from outside Vemoria – she was careful not to say where they were visiting from. She and her father were anxious to find them, to make sure they were all right, to welcome them as honoured guests to her home.

Listening to her speak, you wouldn't have had an idea what was in her mind. Which was a dungeon rather than the best bedroom; the quarries rather than gentle strolls on the lawn.

She didn't have any luck in the mortals' quarter. They weren't interested in much except for their work in hand. They wanted to buy and sell, to make and bake, to craft silver into intricate shapes to sell to the other quarters; to catch the best fish and sell them for the best prices.

Some saw through her story. Some were from Vemoria, and mistrusted anything to do with the First of the Twelve and his friends and relations. Others wondered for a moment if there were anything in it for them; a reward, perhaps.

'Possibly,' said Erica.

Possibly wasn't interesting.

Nonetheless, word spread, people gossiped, mentioned Erica and her questioning to each other. The old nurse stood with her basket, listening, nodding her head in agreement. She didn't look startled at the news, she didn't hurry away so that people had more to talk about. But she cut her shopping short, and she was back home much earlier than usual.

Culun took the news calmly. 'So she hasn't found them either. Good.'

'I thought you wanted them found.'

'Not by her. It's better if I find them.'

'There are others after that Erica,' the nurse said, after a pause.

'Who?'

'Ag and Pag.'

'The Numens?' That made Culun sit up. 'Are you sure?'

The nurse shrugged. 'I don't make things up. I have no imagination. What I say is what I know. It might be right, it might be wrong, but I don't invent. Hiri the baker said that his sister had seen them skulking about. She knows them, because she goes to stay with her husband's family out in the back of beyond. Where the Numens live. They aren't popular, and they don't mix ...'

Culun laughed. 'Tell me something new.'

'... but she knows them well enough to recognize them. And well enough to steer clear of them.'

'Numens ...' said Culun thoughtfully. 'I wonder why they're after Erica.'

'They'll find her,' said the nurse. 'She isn't going to any trouble to keep herself hidden. No subtlety there at all.'

'Get me a cloak,' said Culun. 'I'm going out.'

The Dollop slept the sleep of exhaustion, his big grey sides rising and falling with each breath. Jouri had taken himself off again, still hoping for news of Ben. Hal was at his most irritating, vetoing all Gilly's suggestions of how to pass the time. He whistled tunelessly, and finally tipped some stones out of his pocket on the table and began a complicated game, one hand against the other.

Gilly took out the silver eyes and looked through them. It was a familiar scene, exactly the same as before: the dragon and Ben walking along an unchanging shoreline.

Gilly began to wonder if this image had any reality. Perhaps it was a trick, and she was watching a continuous loop of film with the two figures endlessly walking, never leaving one place, and never getting to another. Gilly shivered and laid the silver eyes on the window sill. She looked at them for a moment, and then picked them up again and put them in her pocket.

'Hal,' she began.

No answer.

Gilly gave up. It's too hot in here, she thought. Hal's no company, I don't know when Jouri will be back, and I'm bored. She went to the door.

'Where are you going?' asked Hal, not looking up from his stones.

'Out,' said Gilly.

'What for?'

'Just to look around. Coming?'

'No,' said Hal.

Gilly sauntered towards the market. She could pass an hour there, easily, looking at the stalls, listening to people bargaining and bartering, watching the parrots preening and screeching. The man with a talking parrot might be there. Then she could go and explore one of the other streets which led off the market square. Or she could go down to the harbour again, see if any fishing boats were coming in.

Shops were opening up after a long break in the heat of the day. They were mostly hole-in-the-wall shops, with merchandise stacked on the pavement, and slower-moving goods within their shadowy interiors.

Gilly lingered at a shop crammed with lamps and lanterns and candle-holders. There was one copper lantern with intricate knotted patterns on it which Gilly liked very much. She leant forward to look more closely at the pattern, which turned out to be leaves entwined with birds and other animals.

It's lovely, she thought, turning to move on.

A shadow fell across her path. For a moment Gilly thought it was the shopkeeper, wanting her to stop so that he could persuade her to buy.

It wasn't. It was a man. A large, plump man wearing a long cloak over his tunic.

Why a cloak in this weather? wondered Gilly. To hide something, a sixth sense told her, as she backed away. A sword?

'Going somewhere?' said the cloaked man. This wasn't a voice Gilly knew, but it made the hairs on the back of her neck stand up. Who was he?

She wasn't going to stay and find out. 'Go away!' she shouted, and at the same moment, taking advantage of his momentary hesitation, she dived past him, and fled away down the street.

He came running after her, but two or three people slowed his progress as they came out of a shop, and Gilly felt for a moment she might escape.

'Not so fast, Gilly,' said an all-too-familiar voice, and Gilly found herself coming to a complete halt, with her arm twisted painfully up behind her back.

'Erica!' said Gilly, struggling to get free. 'Oh, for goodness sake, what a fright you gave me. Let me go.'

'If you struggle, it'll hurt,' said Erica.

It did.

The cloaked man had caught up with them. 'Good,' he said smoothly, stepping forward to pull Gilly away. 'I'll take care of her.'

Erica didn't relax her hold for a moment. 'Scum,' she said, giving Gilly a good shake. All those hours she spent in the gym and the pool back in their world had left their mark, thought Gilly, wincing; she was amazingly strong.

'Careful,' said Culun. 'Your father won't be pleased if you knock her senseless.'

Gilly felt a searing sensation shoot through her brain as it picked up the hostility coming at her from Erica. She reeled, and Erica staggered back. The man reached out to grab her, missed, and in that split second of opportunity, Gilly was off.

Now they were both after her. Gilly kept ahead, twisting and turning, running down tiny streets, hoping that none of them were blind alleys. She had no idea where she was. However will I get back to Hal and Jouri? she thought, as she skidded round a corner.

She found herself in the huge square where they had been when they first arrived in the City. One wide road led off from the centre of the other side. Gilly plunged between the columns, and ran desperately across the square.

Suddenly, there were people around her, waving at her, pointing at something in the ground. A line of pink stone, thought Gilly, what are they on about? Then she stopped as though she had cannoned into a wall of softness. She bounced, in the strangest way, back towards the people who had been shouting at her. And there, grinning at her, was Erica, all ready to seize her again.

Why can't I go across the line? thought Gilly, looking

at it. Nothing there, only the line in the ground. Then she realized. It marked a boundary, and on the other side lived the Immortals and demigods.

'I must get across,' she said urgently to one of the little crowd now gathered round, as she tried to shake herself free of Erica.

'No, you can't.'

'No mortals allowed.'

'Didn't you know that?'

'You have nothing to do with them, and they'll leave you alone.'

'That's right. Best that way.'

The voices broke over her in little waves of sound. Her arm was numb where Erica was holding her, trying to pull her back, away from the line. Then her other arm was snatched by the man in the cloak.

If they both go on tugging, there'll be two of me, thought Gilly. 'Let go, let me go!' she shouted.

She appealed to the people who were drifting away back to their work or shops, the excitement over. 'Help me,' she said. 'These two have no right to hold me.'

'That's nothing to do with us.'

'No, mind your own business, that's best.'

'If you've been up to mischief, you'll have to get yourself out of trouble.'

'Foreigner, aren't you? You should learn our ways before you come here.'

'This way,' said the man.

'Yes, she's coming with us,' said Erica.

Gilly opened her mouth to shout at them, and then, quite suddenly, they relaxed their grips and stepped backwards a pace or two. The crowd began to gather again.

What's happening? thought Gilly. Then she, too,

noticed the figures coming out of one of the huge houses beyond the square, on the Immortals' side.

She stared and stared. It can't be, she said to herself. It just can't be.

It was.

Nineteen

*T*HE TWO MEN WERE WALKING TOWARDS HER, talking. They were both at least eight foot tall. One was dark, with straight black hair. The other had coppery curls and flashing green eyes.

Gilly looked at his neck. Yes, there was a faint jagged line, like an old scar. 'Talking head,' she cried. 'You're the talking head. Only you've joined up with your body again.'

The red-haired giant noticed Gilly for the first time, stopped, and frowned. He didn't seem to like being addressed in this casual way. 'You forget yourself, mortal,' he said arrogantly. 'Keep away from this line, you know better than to cross it.'

Gilly nearly got a crick in her neck looking up at him. 'Hang on,' she said. 'You know who I am!. We saved you, me and Hal.'

'A little mad girl,' said the dark man, as he joined his friend. 'What fun.'

'I'm not mad,' said Gilly hotly.

'Throw her across the square,' he said.

Culun stepped forward to the very edge of the line, and bowed deeply. 'Send her across,' he said. 'We shall deal with her.'

'Do that,' the dark man advised his friend. 'This is all very boring and petty. Leave them to their little squabbles.'

'I need help,' said Gilly.

'And so?' said copper curls.

'You owe me.'

'I *what*?'

Gilly was becoming cross. 'We lugged your head across two countries,' she said indignantly. 'Putting up with your bossy ways and that terrible raven.'

'Lugged your head?' said the dark man, his interest aroused. 'Ril, is this one of the Otherworlders who came to Tuan?'

'It's none of your business,' said green-eyes waspishly.

'And buried it, so that you could get back together with your body again,' Gilly went on relentlessly. 'And it *worked*. Look at you now, hardly a scar to be seen. And when you think how Hal hacked at your neck ...'

Copper-curls shuddered.

'Tell me more,' said the dark man.

'It's none of your business, Siert. It was a private matter.' Ril loomed over Gilly. 'Listen, shorty, I paid my dues. I restored Tuan's magic ...'

'Shorty?' said Gilly, furious. 'I was taller than you when you were just a head in a basket. A dirty head,' she added with satisfaction.

'What?' said Siert. 'Restored Tuan's magic? How? You couldn't do that. You haven't the power.'

'You know nothing about it,' said the ex-head sulkily. 'It involved someone else, the whole sordid business was to do with ... Well, never mind. Someone did have the power, Tuan got its magic back, and the Vemorians had to go back where they'd come from. End of story.'

'If this little sprat did what she said she did, what was her reward?'

Ril shrugged. 'Why should she have any reward?'

'You know the law. She's right, you owe her.'

With a very sour expression on his handsome face, Gilly's erstwhile travelling companion sighed, and addressed Gilly.

'What do you want?'

'Not to be hounded by those two,' she said, pointing at Culun and then at Erica.

'Why are they hounding you?'

'It doesn't matter,' said Gilly. 'I just don't like it.'

Siert eyed Culun. 'He works for the Twelve,' he said. 'Shouldn't be here, but since he is, he's probably up to mischief.' Ril gave Gilly a peeved look. Then he reached out, picked her up by her elbows and dumped her down on his side of the marble strip. 'Come on,' he said. 'I've saved you from that rabble; we'll take you to another place where you can cross back to the mortals' quarter.'

Gilly was open-mouthed as she walked between the tall buildings on either side. She had never seen anything like it in all her life. I wish I had my sketchbook, she thought.

Windows and doors curved, were asymmetrical, had uneven pillars, strange supports. Staircases, twisting and turning in the oddest way, ran up the sides or fronts of many of the houses. The houses were painted in startling colours: azure, lapis lazuli and amethyst purples, embellished with gold and glittering mosaics and tiles. Some had arches leading through to gardens, so full of colour that Gilly reeled from the impact.

These tall beings obviously liked water, which ran along channels built at many levels. There were fountains in the street, attached to houses, visible on balconies. One house even had a cascade pouring down its façade, water that twinkled and sparkled in the sun, and then ran gurgling away into a shell-shaped pool.

'What do the people who live here do?' Gilly asked.

'We have our duties,' said green-eyed Ril.

'Like what?'

'Nosy, your little mortal,' observed Siert. 'If you really want to know, I'm in charge of several wells.'

'In charge of them?'

'I have to make sure that the water flows, and is clean. That it doesn't dry up or become dank or overgrown.'

He doesn't look like a well-cleaner, thought Gilly.

He took instant offence. 'A well-cleaner? I'm a divinity, not a cleaner. I give the wells life. Well-cleaner, indeed. What a nerve.'

Ril sighed. 'Your fault, you were the one who said to rescue her.'

'Where are we going?' asked Gilly. She thought she'd rather not know what Ril did. Something warlike, she felt.

'That's right,' he said. 'Armour. Metals and clothes that protect. Very important,' he added, flashing a green look at his friend.

'Wells are more important,' said Siert.

Gilly had the feeling that this was an old argument. 'Where are we going?' she said again, hoping to distract them.

'I told you, away from your tiresome friends. We'll find a safe place and pass you back to the mortals' quarter. Where you belong.'

And soon, thought Gilly, who was beginning to feel oppressed by the scale and intensity of her surroundings. Even the air she breathed seemed rich and heavy. She longed for something ordinary, everyday.

An answer to her wish flapped across the street, and landed with a hop, skip and a jump in front of them. It was a huge and very black raven, who fixed Gilly with its dark and beady eyes.

Gilly looked, and looked again, and her face broke into a smile. 'Hi,' she said.

'It's you,' squawked the raven, putting its head on one side. 'What a shame, what a shame, what a shame.'

Ril snapped his fingers, and the raven rose with a leisurely flap of its wings to land on his left shoulder. Ril put up a hand to caress its glossy head.

'She's after the Dewstone,' said the raven. 'She and her friends.'

'The Dewstone?' Both men stopped in their tracks and looked at Gilly. 'You? The Dewstone?'

'Don't be silly,' said Gilly. 'I don't know what you're talking about.'

'No mortals' quarter for you,' said green eyes. 'Not until we hear more about this.'

'Where's Gilly?' asked Jouri as he came into the room.

Hal looked up from his stones. 'Oh, she went out. A little while ago.'

'Where to?'

'I don't know. She said she was bored, and went.'

'Why didn't you go with her?'

Hal had been feeling guilty about that. 'I didn't want to,' he said defensively. 'Why should I? She goes off by herself at home.'

'This isn't home,' said Jouri grimly.

'I expect she wanted to wander round the market.'

'I've just come back that way,' said Jouri. 'The place was abuzz with extravagant stories about a chase, and a girl being swept off into the Immortals' zone. A stranger, they said. Not one of us.'

'Could be anyone,' said Hal, trying not to seem worried.

'Could be Gilly. How long ago did she go out, Hal?'

'I didn't really notice,' said Hal. 'I was concentrating on this game.'

'I can see,' said Jouri. 'How long after I went?'

Hal looked uncomfortable. 'Um, not so very long.'

'I've been away for hours.'

Hal looked at Jouri, and Jouri looked at Hal.

Hal swallowed hard, his mouth suddenly very dry. 'What can we do?'

Jouri was thinking. 'We need to find out if it was Gilly, or if she's simply wandering down by the lake. Has she got a good sense of time?'

Hal shook his head. 'None at all,' he said, brightening. Then his face fell again. 'Not hours, though,' he said. 'She wouldn't stay away that long. Even she would realize that she had to get back.'

The Dollop came to life, yawning, arching his back, stretching his legs out.

Hal looked at those large paws with all the claws out, and was glad that he was so friendly. Fully awake now, the Dollop became very alert, his huge whiskers pointed forward, his ears up.

'He knows something,' said Jouri.

'Only we don't know what,' said Hal. 'Gilly seemed to read his mind,' he added 'Couldn't you hypnotize me? In case the same thing happened to me?'

'It doesn't work like that,' said Jouri.

The Dollop padded to the door and sat expectantly beside it.

'Better take him out,' Jouri said to Hal. 'Don't let him out of your sight, and come back quickly. I'll have a word with the innkeeper; he may have heard something.'

It wasn't a case of Hal taking the Dollop, but rather the Dollop taking Hal. He set off down the street at a steady lope, and Hal had to break into a run to catch up with him. 'Stop,' he called.

The Dollop took no notice, but continued on his way, seemingly knowing exactly where he was going. From time to time, he paused to look back as though to check that Hal was following him, and then, with a quick, lithe spring, he was off again.

I do believe he's leading me somewhere, thought Hal. A tiny hope flickered. Could the Dollop possibly know where Gilly was? If Gilly could get pictures from the Dollop's mind, could the Dollop sense where Gilly was?

Hal was across the boundary into the forbidden quarter before he realized. He felt a moment's unease, and then he was running after the Dollop along the wide, quiet, colourful streets.

I shouldn't be here, Hal told himself, but he kept running, anxious not to lose the Dollop, who was far faster than him. Panting, he saw the Dollop swerve through an archway into one of the houses. He swerved, too, bumping his shoulder against the pillar of the arch, and then he was shooting through a courtyard, through another archway, and into a garden.

There were two huge people there, a raven, squawking in an all-too-familiar way, the Dollop, and ...

'Gilly,' he shouted. 'Gilly, are you all right?'

Twenty

*B*EN'S SILENT WORLD WAS STRANGE BUT NOT unpleasant. It was restful not to be able to speak or hear. His mind was becoming quiet, and this brought a strange but pleasant sense of calm. Almost as though my head is floating, he thought.

And, if he couldn't talk, he could smile and gesticulate.

And, moreover, he had a dragon for company.

Tarquin was a dramatic dragon. You could see exactly what he was feeling or thinking by watching his scaly colour changes. Not to mention his rolling eyes, the flames which darted out of his mouth, or the puffs of dark smoke which he could summon up.

And he could dance, and make patterns.

Life, Ben decided, had never been less dull. Even if this peculiar landscape had no beginning and no end, and he was walking under a sun which never rose or set. For one wild moment, Ben even wondered if he was standing still and the scenery all round him was moving, like some gigantic stage set.

So it came as a surprise, a shock, even, when Tarquin landed beside him after one of his soaring jumps, and he heard the swish of his wings. After the silence, the slightest sound seemed enormously amplified, and Ben found his head reeling as the world came rushing back.

He clapped his hands over his ears and shut his eyes, as though that could keep the noise away.

'We're here,' said Tarquin, pleased.

'Where?'

'Here,' said Tarquin irritatingly, gesturing with one of his talons.

A stubborn look came over Ben's face. If Gilly could have seen him now, she wouldn't think of saying he was wet.

'I want to get a few things straight,' he began.

The dragon sighed. 'Must you?'

'Yes. First of all, I want to know where we are. And why I fell into a lake and came ashore from the sea. And why the sound went, and why me?'

'Dear, oh dear,' said the dragon. 'You don't want much, do you? You may not like the answers, but it's entirely up to you.'

'I want to know.'

Tarquin did a quick uncurl of his tail and then snapped it up again in a tighter and more purposeful coil. 'When you fell in the lake,' he said, 'you fell out of time. Because of the egg, you see.'

'Is it the map?'

'It is. Not an ordinary map, though, you understand. You had to make a long journey to get here, where we dragons live.'

Ben looked around him, at the sea, a darker more vigorous, more ordinary sea, and behind them cliffs hundreds of feet high, dotted with cave entrances.

'You live here?'

'We all live here, or hereabouts. In the caves. If you came the normal way, it would take you years to get here. In fact, you never would get here, because it would take about a hundred and fifty years, and you wouldn't be around that long.'

'So how have I got here? A time warp?'

Tarquin gave an approving and sulphurous puff. 'Yes. That's why there was no sound.'

'Okay,' said Ben. 'I believe you.' He paused. 'Is the Dewstone here?'

'It is,' said the dragon.

'With a dragon? Like you?'

'With my uncle,' said Tarquin with pride. 'He's the guardian of the Dewstone. He's been looking after it for centuries.'

Ben knew something about dragons and their treasure. 'Am I supposed to fight him for it?' he asked, thinking that was a bad idea.

Smoke billowed out from Tarquin's mouth and ears as he heaved with laughter. 'You! Fight my uncle! Oh, that's a good one.'

'Is he very fierce?'

'Not as dragons go,' said Tarquin. 'But he's quite large.'

'Ah,' said Ben.

'The Dewstone isn't his,' explained Tarquin. 'I said, guardian. He's looking after it, until the right person comes along to collect it.'

'And that's me?' Ben didn't believe it. 'Just because those two hags sent me?'

'I doubt it,' said Tarquin. 'There's the legend, you see. About a boy with flaming red hair, from another world. I know that's you, because otherwise you would never have found the Tower of Troubles, and your hand wouldn't have opened its door, and you wouldn't have found the egg, and the egg wouldn't have brought you here. No, no, you're the right person. I'm not sure why, but then I don't have to be.'

He looked at Ben intently. 'Is your father like you?'

Ben flushed. 'I haven't got a father.'

'Nonsense. You may not know your father, but you've got one. Have you never seen him?'

'He left, three years ago,' said Ben stiffly.

'Left?'

'Went out for a walk one Sunday morning and never came back.'

'Just vanished, did he?'

'I suppose so.'

'What did your mother think of that?'

'My mother thinks something happened to him,' said Ben. 'She's sure he'll come back one day, as soon as he can.'

'Ha,' said Tarquin. 'Red hair, like you?'

'Yes, actually.'

'Hard on your mother.'

'Yes. Dad didn't earn that much, he was a painter, but it's been very difficult for her, not knowing where he is. She works in London. That's a big city in my country.'

'Yes, go on.'

Ben shrugged. 'She can't have me with her there; it's too expensive and difficult, she says. So I live with my aunt. That's my dad's half-sister.'

'Half-sister, heh? Nice, is she?'

'No,' said Ben. 'She's not.'

'Very interesting,' said the dragon. 'And what do you think? About your father?'

'I hate him,' said Ben at once. 'For going like that.'

'Couldn't help it, I daresay,' said Tarquin. 'I mean, look at you, walking along, minding your own business, a bit of fog, and poof, here you are.'

'That's all very well,' said Ben, 'but what do I do now?'

'Get the Dewstone.'

'And take it back to Ag and Pag.'

'That's the bit I'm not too sure about,' said the dragon. 'It would be much better if those two didn't get their clutches on the Dewstone. In fact, it would be disastrous if they did.'

'They said I had to take it to them. That it was the Law. Otherwise, I'd never get back to my own world.'

'Do you want to?'

Ben opened his mouth to tell Tarquin not to be stupid, and then shut it again. 'I want to see my mother again.'

'Of course you do,' said Tarquin, almost absentmindedly. Then he gave his scales a good shake and became very brisk. 'She wouldn't like it at all, both of you vanishing.'

'It's not the same.'

'How do you know?' said Tarquin. But he didn't give Ben any time to answer. 'Now, come along, we've got things to do.'

'Tarquin,' said Ben. 'How do you get here? Usually? If you live here, and it's so far from the City of Towers and everywhere else.'

'Oh, we dragons go where we want. We don't live in time anywhere, so it's no problem.'

'Oh,' said Ben. He looked up at the towering wall of stone. 'Where do we go from here?'

'Up there; there's no point hanging around at the bottom of a cliff, I would have thought. Of course, it's entirely up to you.'

'No, it isn't,' said Ben with spirit. 'I'm not a mountaineer or a bat or anything that could get up these cliffs. They're sheer, and they seem to go on up for ever.'

The dragon sighed. 'I shall take you up. Climb on my back.'

Ben looked at Tarquin in surprise. 'You've never taken me on your back before.'

'No,' said Tarquin. 'I'm not a horse. But I can see that I'll have to now.'

Those scales looked rough to Ben, and the ones which weren't rough were pointed, and obviously sharp. And how was he to hold on? And could quite a small dragon fly up all that way with a boy clinging to his back?

And ...

'It's entirely up to you,' said Tarquin huffily. 'No spirit of adventure, that's your trouble. And fancy coming all this way and then giving up when faced with a little cliff.'

'It's not a little cliff,' said Ben.

The dragon looked up the cliff and gave a few fiery snorts. 'There are many higher,' he said.

'How do I get on your back?' asked Ben.

'Jump?'

Ben shook his head.

'Stand on a boulder, then.'

Ben looked around him. 'There aren't any boulders.'

'Then you'd better clamber on to my tail and come up that way,' said Tarquin. 'Hurry up; we haven't got all day. And bring that egg with you; it might just come in useful.'

'Got you,' cried Ag with a horrid shriek.

Pag held Erica in an iron grip.

'Let go!' said Erica, furious. 'How dare you ...'

Pag began to shake her. 'Give us our eyes, our silver eyes,' she crooned menacingly. 'Give them to us now, or you'll regret it.'

Half-strangled, Erica managed a high-pitched squeak. 'Silver eyes? I haven't got any silver eyes.'

'A liar,' said Ag.

'I'll shake her until the silver eyes fall out,' decided Pag.

'Yes, and her own eyes and teeth can fall out as well,' cried Ag.

Erica mightn't be a match for two Numens in a temper, but she was a daughter of the Twelve, and a tough cookie in her own right.

Ag retreated, rubbing her arm and uttering dire threats, while Pag's mouth tightened along with her grip.

She thrust her face right up to Erica, who winced at the close-up. 'You came through the barn. You stole our silver eyes from round our necks, while we were sleeping. One each. Give them back.'

'I didn't,' said Erica. 'I came through the barn, yes, but I didn't touch you or steal anything.'

'She isn't afraid,' said Ag regretfully. 'Pag, you aren't hurting her enough.'

'Who else could have taken them?' Pag spat out the words through several teeth which had seen better days.

Erica closed her eyes and gave a contemptuous shudder. 'Perhaps some Otherworlders, the ones I was following. They'd steal anything.'

Ag and Pag stared venomously at their captive. 'Otherworlders? What Otherworlders?'

'Let go of me, and I'll tell you all about them.'

Twenty-One

*H*AL FOUND IT STRANGE TO BE TALKING TO A RIL who had a body as well as a head. He felt a bit awkward about coming face to face with someone he'd only known as a disembodied head. Especially when he noticed the scar on his neck, and he remembered – as he did, all too clearly – how he'd hacked at it …

Hal had the feeling that Ril knew exactly what he was thinking, and he was right.

'Immortals heal without scars,' said Ril scornfully. 'Not like mortals, with their weak bodies. My scar has almost gone, and soon I'll be perfect again.'

That nearly gave Gilly the giggles, but somehow, this wasn't a place for laughter.

'If we hadn't buried your head for you, you wouldn't be in a position to sneer at other people's bodies,' said Hal.

Siert eyed Hal. 'You are brave, mortal,' he said, 'to mock an Immortal.'

'Sorry,' said Hal quickly. No point in starting an argument with a person who came in at about eight foot three. With muscles to match.

'This is Hal,' Gilly said to Siert.

Hal's attention was elsewhere. 'I don't believe it,' he said. 'It's that pesky raven.'

Ril's raven hopped out from behind the fountain. 'Silence in the presence of Immortals,' it cawed.

'Otherwise it'll be the worse for you, what a shame, what a shame, what a shame.'

Hal couldn't help laughing. 'Just the same,' he said. 'Nag, nag!'

'Oh, do be quiet, Hal, and concentrate,' said Gilly. 'They want to know where Ben is, and they're all worked up about the Dewstone.'

'That's the cause of all this trouble,' said Hal. 'And we haven't a clue even what it looks like.'

'The Dollop has,' said Gilly, as a picture flashed into her mind. 'I can see it, not very clearly. It's just a round stone, not very big, with some carvings on it. Almost like runes. There, it's gone.'

'Trouble is right,' said Siert. 'We don't want the Dewstone to be brought back into the world. It's lost, and it should stay lost. Otherwise there'll be a whole heap of trouble. War, civil war, sieges ... and then what about my wells?'

'Might cause some fun,' said Ril, his face brightening. 'You shouldn't always think of yourself.'

'No, I don't,' said Siert. 'Look at the trouble you caused with your meddling.'

'Meddling?' said Hal.

'With mortal affairs,' said Siert coldly. 'You shouldn't get involved with the Tuans and Vemorians, it's unsettling for everyone when Immortals take an interest in mortal affairs.'

'Was that why he was in Tuan?' asked Hal.

'None of your business why I was there.' Ril glared at Hal.

'And one thing leads to another,' said Siert, frowning in a dark and very grand way. 'Now there's unrest brewing in Vemoria, those horrible Numens are up to mischief, which means that the old, Wild Magic may be gathering strength and power. The Tower of Troubles has crumbled into nothingness, so we hear, and who knows where it will end? It's bad for my wells,' he ended pettishly.

'Bad for everyone,' said Ril. 'I don't like it at all, these mists and passing places, and Otherworlders coming through.'

'Especially if one of them is out there after the Dewstone,' put in Siert.

Gilly had to ask. 'Where did the Dewstone come from? And why is it so dangerous and powerful?'

Ril's eyes became a darker green. 'The Dewstone is one of the ancient stones of destiny. The Dewstones were made long ago and far away, when a dying god rolled up the morning dew from the fields of time and breathed all his power into them.'

'Dewstones? In the plural?' said Hal.

'There were five. Four are lost for ever. One remains.'

'Where?'

'No one knows, but the legend said it would be found again, and taken from its keepers, and brought back. By a boy with red hair, from another world. From the line of the Old Kings, interestingly enough. Possibly your friend.'

'Tiresome boy,' remarked the raven. 'He's gone to find the Dewstone because Ag and Pag sent him off.'

Ril looked the raven in the eye. 'Are you sure?'

'Caw,' said the raven. 'Silly boy, ate an apple, what a shame, what a shame, what a shame.' It flapped its black wings a few times, and landed heavily on the top of the fountain. A chip of marble fell off and tumbled into the water.

Ril sighed, but the raven took no notice. 'The boy's gone walkies with a dragon, everyone knows that.'

'Everyone doesn't,' said Siert, much interested. 'For instance, I don't.'

'You don't hang around the markets like my raven does,' said Ril. 'Picks up a lot of gossip and news. Very useful.'

'If you spent less time on all that, you'd be further up the hierarchy,' said Siert.

Ril shrugged. 'It doesn't matter to me,' he said. 'I enjoy myself, what's wrong with that? And,' he added, his face lighting up, 'I love gossip and news.' Then the dissatisfied expression came back. 'And it's not my fault I haven't got much to do. There aren't enough wars, and hardly any fighting at the moment, so I've hardly got any armour or weapons to look after. I would have more to do if the big cheeses over on the island got off their bums and did a bit of work.'

'Disrespectful,' said Siert half-heartedly. 'Insulting the gods. They have other things to think about, they'll get round to war in due course.'

'Like, in a few thousand years?' said Ril.

'Plenty of time.'

Hal and Gilly looked at each other. 'Pinch me,' whispered Gilly. 'We must be dreaming.'

'No way,' said Hal, nonetheless obliging with a forceful pinch.

'Ouch,' said Gilly. 'No, I didn't say anything,' she added hastily, as Siert and Ril stared at her.

'We need to find your little friend, the supposed Red One,' said Siert. 'Before he hands the Dewstone over to Ag and Pag.'

'That's what Lugh said.'

Ril and Siert stiffened. 'Lugh? Lugh the Soothsayer?' said Ril. 'Huh, I remember him.'

'Ag and Pag?' asked Hal.

'Numens,' said Siert. 'Immortals, but beyond the

pale. They don't live in the City, but out in the back of beyond. No one can bear having them around, and they have ties to the Wild Magic, which isn't approved of.'

Ril pursed his lips and shook his head. 'Can't interfere with the mortal boy,' he said. 'He's bound to Ag and Pag if he ate one of their apples, and that's that.'

'If Ag and Pag get hold of the Dewstone, they'll use it to unloose a chaos of Wild Magic,' said Siert. 'We can't have that.'

'Make a bargain with the Numens,' said Ril. 'The only problem is, you've got nothing to bargain with.'

Siert looked hard at Gilly. 'Why have you got that blank look on your face? You're tuning in to the Dollop here, aren't you?' He paused, and frowned. 'In fact, it isn't just the Dollop. You can see more than that, can't you?'

Gilly hesitated, and was lost.

'Ah, you can.' Siert's eyes narrowed. 'How? Come on, out with it.'

Hal shook his head at Gilly, but she had no choice. 'Silver eyes,' she said.

They were transfixed.

'Silver eyes?' said Ril. 'You see through silver eyes? Where did you get them from?'

'A ... friend,' said Gilly warily. 'He gave them to me.'

'And where,' demanded Siert, 'did he get them from?'

'From the Numens.'

'Liar,' said Ril coldly. 'She's lying. No Numen ever gave up her silver eye. Horrible old hags,' he added for good measure.

Gilly flushed. 'I'm not sure how this friend got them. But he can't see anything through them, and I can.'

'So,' said Siert.

'Okay, you snivelling little mortal, what do you see?' Ril took a step nearer to Gilly, who shrank back.

'There's no need to threaten,' said Siert, strumming his great fingers on the stone balustrade round the fountain. 'Because Gilly is going to tell us exactly what she can see, aren't you, little mortal? And she's going to tell us now.'

Twenty-Two

*B*EN HAD A SENSATION OF BEING WATCHED. THAT slight tingling at the back of the neck, which makes you turn round to see who's looking at you.

There was no one there; hardly surprising when you were at the mouth of a cave hundreds of feet up the sheer side of a cliff.

He wasn't to know it was Gilly who was watching him from an immeasurable distance. Watching through her silver eyes. Nor that one look at the cliff and the silver eyes fell from her face, leaving her sitting queasily on the edge of a fountain.

The cave smelt. Of animal, and fire, and herbs and age. Underfoot, it was soft and mossy; within, it was very dark and very quiet. There was just a single huge yellow light suspended as though by magic some sixty feet in the air.

However high is this cave? thought Ben, as the yellow lamp blinked, went dark, gleamed out again from the darkness. 'It isn't a lamp,' he said aloud.

'What?' said Tarquin.

'The yellow light.'

'It's my uncle's eye,' said Tarquin, briskly. 'I expect he's snoozing as usual.'

Ben's own eyes were becoming accustomed to the darkness. He was beginning to be able to make out some shapes. Chiefly one shape. Rocks? Boulders? And whatever size head did Tarquin's uncle have if that was his eye?

Ben was starting to realize that Uncle Dragon came in the large economy size. Nothing prepared him for the reality revealed as Tarquin flew around the cave, breathing jets of flame and lighting a series of flares set into the walls. It was a meagre light, but enough for Ben to see a dragon more enormous than anything he could have imagined.

This dragon was bigger than the biggest cathedral Ben had ever seen. He was as big as all his school buildings heaped together. You could have driven to the top of him and parked rows and rows of cars and coaches and still had space to roam around.

This dragon was seriously big.

He was, Ben thought as he peered into the shadows, mostly a red dragon. With quite a lot of gold and bronze.

'Over here,' said Tarquin, propelling Ben to one side. 'Otherwise you might get a bit scorched.' He stood beside Ben, his tail neatly coiled. 'Let's wake him up properly.'

Tarquin might be a very small dragon indeed compared to his uncle, but his dragon's roar was coming along nicely. It was loud enough to penetrate the big dragon's sleep. A vast mouth opened in a great and toothy yawn. Ben eyed the teeth with respect. They would have come in handy when Stonehenge was being built.

A rumble filled the cave, followed by a torrent of flames. Ben shrank back against the wall, but Tarquin took no notice. 'This is the Red One, Uncle,' he shouted. 'Come for the Dewstone.'

Another vast rumble filled the cave.

'He says he's not giving up the Dewstone,' said Tarquin.

'That's that, then,' said Ben. 'Best be off.'

'Well, if you've come all this way just to give up,' said Tarquin, aggrieved. 'I can tell you how to get the Dewstone, but of course if you'd rather stay being Ag and Pag's kicking boy for the rest of your days … Well, it's entirely up to you.'

Ben reluctantly stayed where he was. 'Okay,' he said with a sigh. 'What do I have to do?'

'Make him laugh,' said Tarquin.

'Make him *laugh*?' Ben couldn't believe his ears.

'Yes, you know: ho, ho, ho.'

'And how do I do that?' said Ben. 'It's not the sort of thing you learn at school. There's no Module 3B, Making Dragons Laugh.'

'How do you make people at school laugh?' enquired Tarquin.

Just show my face, thought Ben gloomily.

'All right, how do normal people make other people laugh?'

'They tell jokes.'

'Go on, then.'

'What kind of jokes?'

'Dragon jokes.'

Gilly and Hal walked quickly through the dark alleys of the mortals' quarter. The Dollop padded a little way in front on soft grey feet, going more slowly now, but unhesitatingly choosing this or that narrow alley to take.

'How does he know?' whispered Gilly.

'More blinking magic,' said Hal crossly. 'I hate this place, I hate all these peculiar people, I wish I was back home in my own room. Lying on my bed. Doing nothing. With Ben waiting for us the next morning, to walk to school.'

'No chance,' said Gilly. 'We have to find Ben.'

'I know, I know; but then what? What's Ben going to do when he realizes he's got a stone of power or whatever it is? Mind you, I don't believe a word of it.'

'You didn't last time,' said Gilly mildly.

The Dollop increased speed and loped round the corner. There was the inn, its sign swinging in the breeze.

'Clever Dollop,' said Gilly.

'Uh uh,' said Hal, as the Dollop came to an abrupt halt, the hairs on his back rising in a bristly frenzy. His tail bushed out to an enormous size, his ears lay flat on his head.

'What's up?' said Gilly.

Then she knew, as angry signals from the Dollop flooded into her mind, wavering into a clear picture of a person she knew all too well.

'Erica,' she said. 'I don't believe it. The Dollop can sense Erica.'

'Just Erica?' asked Hal.

'No. Unfortunately I get the impression that one of the Twelve's with her. The terrible, dark, grim man. The one we saw with her in our world.'

'Mmm,' said Hal. He looked up and down the deserted street. 'Scarper time, I think.'

'What about Jouri?'

'I don't expect Jouri's hanging around waiting to offer Erica a nice cup of tea. Come on, Gilly. Move!'

They got to the end of the alleyway and turned to look back to the inn. At that very moment Erica and Uthar came out of the inn door, followed by two not-very-pleasant looking women.

'After them,' shrieked Ag.

'Get them,' screeched Pag.

Gilly would never forget the terror of that chase. It was like a nightmare come alive, and her fear of the figures behind them gave her feet wings. As for Hal, his sports master would never have believed that Hal could run so fast.

Not fast enough. No matter how fast they ran, no matter how many times they twisted and ducked into new alleys, the pursuers were there.

And they were gaining on them.

'Keep going, Gilly,' panted Hal. 'They can't keep this up.'

They could.

They ran, lungs bursting, down a wide, cobbled street. It was now quite dark, and lights from the dwellings on either side spilled eerily on to the uneven surface. They clattered to the end, and then stopped in horror, looking out over the black water which lapped against a jetty.

'The lake,' said Gilly in despair.

'Back,' shouted Hal.

'We can't.'

Their pursuers were only metres behind them, sure of their triumph. Then Dollop gave a roar and launched himself into the water.

'Hal,' cried Gilly. 'He can't swim. He'll drown.' And she leapt in after the big grey Dollop, heedless of the dark and the chill grimness of the water.

With one desperate look behind him, Hal jumped too, swimming desperately towards the Dollop.

Who was swimming.

'I thought you said he couldn't swim,' said Hal, spluttering in the cold water.

'He can,' said Gilly, intent on what was floating into her mind. 'He doesn't *want* to. He couldn't last time because it was too far. He's going away from the shore. And then back; he knows that we can get ashore further along.'

'They'll catch us before that,' said Hal, swimming strongly to keep up with the Dollop.

'No,' said Gilly. 'Look!'

For a moment they paused, looking back to the jetty. Ag and Pag were doing a frenzied dance of rage. Uthar was trying to untie an ancient dinghy which was moored to a big metal ring.

'They must be witches of some kind,' said Gilly. 'And witches can't cross flowing water.'

'Is this flowing?'

'Feel the current.'

'And what about Erica? She can swim, she's some kind of a champion.'

'Maybe in a pool. Maybe she's not about to plunge into dark water like this. Maybe she can't see us.'

'Maybe if we move, we can lose them entirely.'

'How does a lazy dragon get down from a tree?'

'Flies. Easy.'

'No. Sits on a leaf and waits for autumn.'

All the great scales rattled, as the huge and ancient dragon shook with mirth. 'Go on. More.'

'How do you know if a dragon's been in ...' Ben panicked. In a fridge? This dragon wouldn't know what a fridge was. Improvise, he told himself. 'In the larder?'

Pause, for dragon thought.

'Well?'

'Footprints in the butter.'

Tarquin thought that one was very funny, which

—— 173 ——

made Ben wonder if the little dragon – as he now thought of him – had raided the odd larder in his time.

'How do you know if there's a dragon in your bed?'

'Go on.'

'By the "D" on his pyjamas.'

If that dragon rumbles and shakes much more, thought Ben, he's going to cause an earthquake.

'Any more?' said Tarquin, who was grinning as dragons do, with little puffs of smoke and jets of blue and red flames spurting out from between his rows of teeth.

'Why do dragons paint their toenails red?'

'Mmm,' said the big dragon. 'Why?'

'So that they can hide in cherry trees.'

'Calm down, Uncle,' said Tarquin. 'You'll do yourself a mischief.'

The great dragon subsided with a few comparatively minor heaves, and a majestic burst of flame.

'Hmm,' he said. 'Any more?'

Ben thought hard. 'What do you call a dragon with his claws in his ears?'

'A foolish dragon,' said uncle, after a moment's thought.

'No, anything you like, because he can't hear you.'

'Oh, very good, very good,' said the dragon, smoke and flames spiralling out of his mouth.

'Uncle?' said Tarquin.

The dragon looked down at the two small figures standing by his huge and scaly claw. 'It's yours,' he said. 'Over there.'

He indicated a spot of darkness in the wall by sending an arrow of flame towards it.

'Leave this to me,' said Tarquin, edging round the dragon's foot.

Keeping close to the wall, and with a wary eye on his

uncle, Tarquin sidled round to the dark place. He blew softly at it, there was a sudden brilliant flash of light, and then a glowing ball lay in his carefully curled talons.

Tarquin came back, never taking his eyes off his uncle, who seemed quite uninterested in the proceedings.

'There,' he said, holding it out to Ben.

Ben looked at it. 'Is it luminous?' he asked in a whisper.

'It glows, yes.'

'Is it the Dewstone?'

'Yes, it's the Dewstone all right.'

'It's very small.'

'You don't have to be big to be effective.'

'I think your uncle should keep it.'

Ben couldn't have explained his reluctance to reach out and take the stone. After all, the big dragon had said he could have it, and it wasn't doing Tarquin any harm.

'We've come all this way, and now you won't have it,' said Tarquin. 'Most inconsiderate, but of course, it's entirely up to you. Won't ever get a second chance, you know.'

Then the other dragon stirred and spoke. No warm rumbles now, just a cold voice that seemed to come out of time.

'Take it, Red One. You have no choice. I liked the jokes. It takes courage for a boy to joke with a dragon, and you'll need courage when you have the Dewstone. Courage, and a good heart. Guard it while you have it, keep it when the bargain is made, and then you must decide ...'

The echoing voice faded into the cave. 'Decide ... cide ... ide ...'

'Decide what?'

There was a long silence, and then Tarquin spoke. 'He's gone to sleep again. Take it, Ben. You have to.'

Ben stretched out a hand, hesitated, held it out firmly. He gave a little sound of surprise as it dropped into his palm. 'It's burning,' he said, nearly dropping it. 'And it's so heavy!'

'Only for a moment,' said Tarquin. 'Let it get used to you, and it won't seem hot or heavy.'

Ben blinked and looked down at the Dewstone. 'It's carved,' he said. 'With strange signs.'

Tarquin squinted at it. 'It would be,' he said. 'That's the old tongue of the Thirdlands, when the world and the gods were a lot younger than they are now. I expect it's the name of the god who made the Dewstones. Don't *worry* so,' he added in a burst of irritation. 'You don't have to understand everything about a stone of power.'

'What *is* this power the Dewstone has?'

'Ah,' said Tarquin. 'Best not to enquire.'

Twenty-Three

GILLY, HAL AND THE DOLLOP CAME ASHORE IN A quiet, dark inlet where there were no streets, no houses, and no people. And no Vemorians or Numens.

'Thank goodness,' said Gilly, as she waded, dripping, from the water's edge and collapsed on the sand. 'I'm whacked. I'm not used to swimming that far.'

Hal, who complained furiously every week when the swimming coach made him swim length after length, felt comfortably superior. 'Stamina,' he said. 'That's what counts.'

'Like. when we went on the charity walk and you gave up after six miles?'

'That was different.'

'Now what?' said Gilly, too tired to go on arguing. She squeezed her hair in an attempt to get some of the water out and shook her head to ease her waterlogged ears.

The Dollop stood firmly on his big paws and shook himself, sending a shower of water over Gilly and Hal.

'Hey!' said Hal crossly. 'Cats,' he added in an undertone. 'Typical.'

The Dollop took no notice, but embarked on the calm and seemingly endless washing essential to all members of the cat family when wet.

'Oh, come *on*,' said Hal.

'Leave him be,' said Gilly. 'Cats don't like being wet.'

'Nor do I.'

'Run about, get dry that way.'

Hal gave his sister a scornful look and plumped down on the sand beside her. The moon had risen while they were swimming and now shone huge and round in the sky. The lake glowed in its pale light. 'At least we can see now,' said Hal.

'Nothing to see,' said Gilly.

Hal sat up. 'Oh no? I can hear something rustling.'

'Where?'

'Over there.'

He pointed to some bushes which grew in a huddle on the sloping bank behind them. 'Ssh,' he said, even though Gilly hadn't made a sound. 'There it is again.'

'The Dollop's heard it,' said Gilly, looking over to where the big cat sat motionless, one leg raised behind an ear. Then the Dollop relaxed and went back to his methodical washing.

'It's Jouri,' exclaimed Gilly.

'What do you mean, it's Jouri? You can't see who it is, any more than I can.'

'The Dollop knows it's Jouri,' said Gilly firmly.

And it was. He slid out of the bushes, and came noiselessly over the sand towards them. 'Okay?' he asked in a soft voice.

'Yes,' said Hal, in a normal voice. 'Where have you been?'

'Not so loud,' said Jouri. 'Sound carries over water. And who knows …'

Gilly looked out at the still water, half expecting Erica and Pag to come surging out of the shadows like marauding Vikings.

'What now?' she asked in a whisper.

'Off to meet Ben,' said Jouri.

'Ben?' said Hal.

—— 178 ——

'Ssh,' said Gilly and Jouri together.

Hal dropped his voice. 'Where is he?' he said. 'Where's he been? Was Gilly right, when she said she saw him standing in a cave halfway up a cliff?'

'She was,' said Jouri. 'He'll be back, after dawn, when the dragons have flown.'

'Flown where?'

'Where they fly at dawn,' said Jouri unhelpfully. 'Ben will come back to the City of Towers.'

'With this Dewstone?'

'I hope so.'

'How do you know all this?'

'Sources,' said Jouri.

'Sources?' said Hal suspiciously.

Gilly poked him in the ribs. 'Spies have sources,' she whispered. 'That's their job.' Then she looked hard at Jouri. There was something different about him. 'Jouri! Whatever happened to your eyebrows? They're singed.'

'He's been talking to a dragon,' said Hal with a crack of laughter.

'Exactly so,' said Jouri.

Ag and Pag were in conference. They had watched Erica and Uthar sail out on to the lake and out of sight.

'They won't find them,' said Ag.

'Not a chance,' agreed Pag.

'Hope they drown,' added Ag.

'No, Uthar will be useful to us. When we have the Dewstone and leave the Thirdlands to have some fun.'

'He wants the Dewstone.'

'He can't have it. It's ours,' said Pag.

'If the boy hands it over.'

Pag was complacent. 'He has to,' she said.

'How do we know he has it?'

'We don't, because those mortals have stolen our eyes. But he will have succeeded, if he is the Red One.'

'And if he isn't?'

'Stupid,' hissed Pag. 'Of course he is.'

'Yes, yes,' said Ag, backing away. 'Are we going to wait for the boat to come back?'

'No.'

'What then?'

'Shut up. I'm thinking.'

Thinking wasn't something Ag did much of, so she lapsed into a malevolent stupor, while Pag's more agile brain clicked away.

Some time later, Pag gave a breathy sigh, and a nasty sniff. 'Got it,' she said. 'That boy will be on his way back. When it's daylight. He'll meet up with his friends if he can.'

'He should come straight to us.'

'How can he, idiot? He doesn't know where we are.'

'We don't know where he is.'

'We can find out.'

'How? We were relying on our silver eyes. Without them, we're helpless. What can we do? He could be anywhere. How can we find him?'

'Ways and means,' said Pag viciously. 'Leave it to me.'

Ag licked her lips. 'Can't I watch?'

'Quicker if you don't,' said Pag.

'Are you sure Ben is coming back?' asked Gilly as they walked quickly along a deserted but moonlit track. 'And when?'

'The dragon told me,' said Jouri.

Hal eyed Jouri suspiciously. He wasn't at all sure about these dragons. He hadn't believed in dragons since he was four years old. On the other hand, there was the talking head, that was strange enough. Not to mention the Dollop. Well, he'd keep an open mind.

'If you know about Ben,' he asked Jouri, 'what about other people? Does anyone else know he's on his way back? With this Dewstone thing?'

'I hope not,' said Jouri, a slight frown crossing his brow. 'It was a private place, and no one was there, as far as I know.'

Gilly's instincts were acute in a way they never had been. 'You aren't sure,' she said at once. 'You've got a feeling someone was there, someone who might have heard what you did.'

'Just a feeling,' said Jouri. 'I looked, there was no one to be seen.'

'There's nothing we can do about it in any case,' said Hal. 'Is it far, Jouri?' He stifled a huge yawn.

'Not far, no,' said Jouri. 'When we get there you can have a nap. There's a little while to go until dawn.'

'Is dawn special?' asked Gilly.

'The dragons fly at dawn,' said Jouri. 'I told you.'

'Dragons,' said Hal, kicking a stone out of his way. 'Dragons, indeed.'

Ben stood alone at the foot of the cliff. Above him the air was dark and full of the sound of great wings as the dragons came out of their lairs and took to the skies. To the east, the sky was changing as he watched from palest pink to a fiery red, then yellow, then a blaze of purple.

There was a clap of thunder as the sun began to edge up over the horizon, and the sky faded to a clear blue; aquamarine tinged with the blue of Greek islands.

Ben was lost in wonder. Nothing could ever be so marvellous as this. He put his hand in his pocket to feel the Dewstone, cooler now, but still possessed of a life of its own. There goes Tarquin, he said to the Dewstone, as the smaller dragons joined in the whirling dragon dance. And who would have thought that Tarquin's uncle, clearly visible as the biggest and grandest of all the dragons, could be so graceful?

Nothing, he thought with awe, will ever be the same again. Not now I've seen dragons flying at dawn.

His old nurse let Culun into the house. She had a very sour expression on her face. 'They're upstairs,' she said, with a jerk of her head. 'Arguing.'

Culun sidled into the gloomy upstairs room where Uthar and Erica, wet and angry after their futile pursuit, were shouting furiously at each other.

'Hem,' he said politely.

They took no notice.

He tried again. 'Uh hem!' he said.

No good. He stepped forward and raised his voice. 'My lord Uthar!'

That stopped them. They stared at him, two pairs of cold, dark eyes raking him over.

'Well?' said Uthar. 'Why are you interrupting our discussion?'

'News,' said Culun. 'About the boy, and the Dewstone. Of course, if you wish, I will withdraw, and wait for you outside.' He gave a fat bow and pretended to move back to the door.

'Stop,' said Uthar in his unfriendly way. 'Out with it.'

'Where is he?' said Erica eagerly. 'And any news of the others?'

'They are together,' said Culun. 'Or will be, shortly. I overheard the man who was with them, Jouri the Gonelander, talking to a dragon.'

'A dragon? Ha,' said Uthar. 'Go on. What else?'

Culun shrugged. 'Nothing else. This man and, I

suppose, his two travelling companions, the Earth-dwellers, are going to meet the red-haired boy at the Place of the Winds. At daybreak.'

'At daybreak.' Uthar glanced out of the window. The first pale lightening of dawn was visible in the eastern sky.

'Is it far from here?' said Erica.

'Not so far,' said Culun, who wasn't at all sure how far it was. 'You leave the City of Towers by the Western gate, and keep going. So I was told.'

'We must go at once,' said Uthar.

'Where are Ag and Pag?' asked Erica, as she swept towards the door.

Culun raised his shoulders. 'Who knows? Plotting in some dark alleyway.'

'Disgusting creatures,' said Erica.

Twenty-Four

TARQUIN ZOOMED AND SWOOPED ACROSS THE SKY above the borderlands between the Thirdlands and Vemoria, making Ben wish he had some pills you could take for dragon-sickness. Wedged between the dragon's wings, he knew he couldn't fall off, but even so, the ground seemed a long, long way down.

He tried to shout a question at the dragon, but with the rush of the wind, and the steady beat of Tarquin's wings, his words were lost in the air.

There was a bank of clouds ahead, and Ben ducked instinctively as Tarquin plunged into the white mass. The mist streamed past him, and then fell away as the dragon came out once more into the clear blue sky. I hope we get there soon, thought Ben. This method of travelling is all very well, but it isn't exactly comfortable.

At that very minute Tarquin did a nosedive towards the ground. Ben's ears popped as he hung on for dear life. Then the dragon relented, slowed his speed and came down towards the earth in a series of lazy loops.

At first Ben couldn't make out anything below them, but then he could see some buildings, and streets, and a pattern of fields and woods. Then they were out in the country again, and there, a good way away, but visible, was a solitary hill with a tower perched on the very top.

And by the tower were three familiar figures, and a large animal.

'The Dollop,' cried Ben. 'Oh, it's the Dollop.'

He was so excited to see his friends once more that he looked no further. If he had, he would have seen Erica and Uthar approaching from the west, and, closer to the hill on the other side, Ag and Pag toiling up the slope, their long and shapeless garments flapping about them in the strong winds.

Below, the Dollop was the first to know that something was amiss. He flashed vivid images at Gilly, first of the Vemorians, and then of the Numens.

'Jouri,' said Gilly in an urgent voice. 'Jouri, they're here. Erica and that one of the Twelve, and those two horrible women from the barn.'

'Together?' asked Jouri.

Gilly closed her eyes, and concentrated. 'I don't think so,' she said cautiously. 'They're coming from different directions.' She became more definite. 'The women are nearer.'

'Go into the tower,' said Jouri. 'Wait for Ben. I'll go and see what I can do, I may be able to draw the Vemorians off. The Dollop can come with me, he'll be good at this kind of thing.'

Jouri set off down the hill at a brisk run, the Dollop loping alongside him with easy strides.

'Are you sure they're coming?' asked Hal, as he and Gilly crept inside the remains of the tower.

Gilly nodded.

Hal looked up into the mass of crumbling brickwork interspersed with branches and brambles. 'There's a tree growing right up the centre of the tower,' he said.

'The tower must be very old,' said Gilly, 'for the tree to be so big. I wonder what it was for, out in the middle of nowhere like this.'

'There'll be something weird about it,' said Hal

morosely. 'Like everything else in this country. It makes even Vemoria seem quite ordinary.'

'No, it doesn't,' said Gilly. 'Just remember the quarries.'

Hal preferred not to remember the quarries. He peered out from a narrow slit in the stonework, craning his neck to scan what he could of the surrounding countryside. 'No sign of Ben,' he said. 'No sign of anyone. Are you sure you're right about the others? Are they getting closer.'

'I can't tell,' said Gilly. 'The Dollop must be too far away.'

'Wish Jouri hadn't gone off like that,' grumbled Hal. 'Leaving us here without a clue as to what's going on.'

'Quiet,' said Gilly.

'Why?'

'I can hear something. A kind of creaking.'

'Creaking?' echoed Hal. 'What do you mean, a kind of a creaking? Where?'

'Above us,' said Gilly. 'Listen, it's getting closer.'

A dark shadow passed above the top of the ruined tower, making the two of them duck.

'What is it?' said Hal, recovering himself. 'Some kind of eagle.'

'No,' said Gilly in awed tones. 'Not an eagle. Oh, look, Hal. It's a dragon.'

'I don't believe it,' began Hal, and then forgot his doubts as a familiar small figure slid down to the ground and stood beside what was unquestionably a dragon. Not a very big dragon, but a dragon.

'Ben,' yelled Gilly, forgetting to be cautious. She was out of the tower like a shot, running towards Ben. 'Thank goodness you're safe.'

'Hi, Gilly,' said Ben. 'Hi, Hal. Where's the Dollop? I saw her from up there. Oh, this is Tarquin,' he added proudly, introducing his friend, who had coiled his tail and calmed his scale-colour down to a peaceful bronze tone.

'A real dragon,' said Gilly, walking round him.

Tarquin belched a few flames. 'Sorry,' he said. 'I'm not used to passengers. I think I've got hiccups.'

'Have a glass of water,' said Hal unhelpfully.

'Try very hard not to think of the word hippopotamus,' urged Gilly.

Tarquin fixed her with a startled eye. 'That's impossible,' he said. 'How can I try not to think of a word? By trying not to think about it, I can't help thinking about it. And why a hippopotamus? I never think about hippopotamuses, not from one year's end to another.'

'There,' said Gilly. 'You see, it's worked. Your hiccups have gone.'

Tarquin blew a few experimental puffs of smoke and fire. 'Good gracious, she's quite right. Remarkable. Who would have thought there was such power in a hippopotamus? I must tell my uncle about this.'

'It's not exactly the word hippopotamus,' Gilly began, and gave up. 'As long as it worked,' she finished.

'Ho,' said the dragon. 'I don't like to mention it, Ben, but those Numens are just coming over the brow of the hill. I fancy they want the Dewstone. I wouldn't hand it over, speaking personally, but of course, it's entirely up to you.'

Ag and Pag came flapping and panting up the hill, their eyes glinting in a threatening and evil way. 'Go away, horrible dragon. Be off,' said Ag, slapping at Tarquin as she arrived breathless at the foot of the tower.

'He has to give it to us,' said Pag, her eyes gleaming in expectation. 'If he doesn't want to say goodbye to his friends right now. Forever. The Law's the law, and you can't change that, not for all your posh dragon uncles.'

'Is she right?' asked Ben. Now that the moment had come, he felt very reluctant to hand the Dewstone over. He fingered it in his pocket. He felt very strongly that the Dewstone shouldn't be given to the Numens, that it didn't want to be handed over, and that they would misuse it terribly ... But what choice did he have?

'None,' said Ag, advancing on him, her claw-like hands held out for the Dewstone.

Ben retreated, hating their greedy eyes, sure that to give them the Dewstone would be wrong, would have terrible consequences. But what could he do? A picture of his mother floated into his mind.

'You see, you see, there's nothing you can do, give it to me, give it to me,' shrieked Pag. 'Power, power, all ours.'

'If it's got such power,' said Hal, 'can't Ben use it to turn these two into stone or something?'

'Sadly, not,' said the dragon. 'It's Ben's because he was the one destined to reclaim it from the dragons, but he has to give it up, because of his bond with the Numens.'

'They tricked me,' said Ben. 'They *made* me eat that apple.'

'Give it to us, give it to us, it's your own fault, you have to hand it over.' Ag and Pag were becoming alarmed by the delay.

'Of course, you can bargain, you know,' said Tarquin to Ben, in a casual kind of way.

'Bargain?'

'Yes. You may have something they want more than the Dewstone. That they'd take instead of the Dewstone. Of course, it's entirely up to you.'

'I haven't got anything that they'd want,' said Ben.

'Look, the only thing I've got apart from the Dewstone is these.' He pulled his glasses out of his other pocket and showed them to Tarquin. 'They'd hardly swap the Dewstone for my specs, would they?'

'Nearly right,' said Tarquin. 'After all, what use would Numens have for glasses? They have their silver eyes to see with.'

Pag curled her lip at the dragon in a nasty snarl. 'Our eyes have been stolen, and when we have the Dewstone, we'll get them back.'

'Yes,' agreed Ag. 'We'll use the Dewstone to blast those Vemorians and get our eyes back.'

'You see,' said Tarquin, in a very relaxed and chatty way, 'Numens can do very little without their silver eyes. They only get one each, when they're dragged into the world. If it's lost, that's it, really.'

Ag gave a whimper. 'We'll get them back, we will, we will.'

'Shut up,' said Pag. 'What do you know about our silver eyes?' she asked Tarquin menacingly. 'Tell us, or it'll be bad luck for the boy.'

'I know where they are,' said Tarquin. 'You can have them back if you give up the Dewstone.'

'Shan't,' said Pag at once.

'Won't,' said Ag.

'Very well,' said Tarquin, quite unbothered.

He's up to something, thought Gilly, who was longing to check that the eyes were safely in her own pocket. She didn't dare, those two would notice if she made the slightest move.

'Where's the Dewstone, then?' Tarquin went on. 'Bring it out, Ben, so that the Numens can see it. It won't be much use to them, if they don't have their eyes. It's the eyes that allow them to get up to so much mischief and malice, you see. It's what connects them to

the old magic. It's going to be strange, isn't it?' he said
to Ag and Pag. 'No eyes, no Wild Magic. Won't life be
dull?'

'All right.' Pag gave in, hissing and breathing with a
horrid, rasping sound. 'We want our eyes. Tell us where
our eyes are.'

'Set Ben free,' said Tarquin. 'Release him from his
bond.'

'How do we know you'll stick to your side of the
bargain?'

Tarquin sent out a spurt of angry flames. 'We
dragons,' he said, affronted, 'keep our word.'

Pag shot him a look of utter hatred, and grabbed Ag
by the hand. She reached out and held Ben's arm with
her other hand. Then the two of them chanted some
unintelligible sounds, and she dropped Ben's arm with
an extra shove which sent a pain shooting up to his
shoulder. 'Ouch,' he said.

'That'll teach you,' said Ag.

Pag was standing in front of Tarquin. 'Well? Our
eyes?'

Tarquin nodded at Gilly. 'Give them back, Gilly.'

Gilly reached into her pocket as Pag exploded in a
frenzy of rage.

'*She* had them. All the time. *She* had them. We could
have got them off her just like that. We've been tricked.
Give us the Dewstone, it's ours, it's ours.' Her voice
rose to a pitch of frenzy and fury.

'No chance,' said Tarquin. 'You released Ben, no
going back on that. There's no way you can have the
Dewstone now, none at all. Ben is its guardian now, so
be off with you.'

Gilly watched in fascination as a ripple of dark red
quivered along Tarquin's scales.

'He's changing colour,' she said.

'He's angry,' said Hal, who was secretly very impressed by the dragon, even if he wasn't about to admit it. 'He's got the better of them; well done, Tarquin. And well done, Ben,' he added.

Ag and Pag were uttering a stream of terrible sounding words, hatred gleaming out of their eyes as they glared at Ben.

'What are they saying?' Ben asked nervously.

'They're just cursing you,' said Tarquin. 'Saying that because you've tricked them, you'll never see your father again.'

Ben nearly jumped out of his skin. 'My *father*? What has my father got to do with it?'

'This and that,' said Tarquin. 'Don't worry, Ben, they can't hurt you or anyone else now that you've got the Dewstone.' He shot a ball of fire in the Numens' direction. 'Be off with you.'

Ag and Pag went off down the hill in a series of discontented hops and jumps, wailing and lamenting at every step.

'Time for breakfast, I think,' said Tarquin, settling his scales back into position. 'I'm extremely hungry.'

Twenty-Five

'NOT JUST YET,' HAL SAID REGRETFULLY; HE WAS hungry, too. 'We've got to find Jouri. He's with the Dollop, he went off to see what Erica and Uthar are up to.'

'Uthar,' said Tarquin. 'The First of the Twelve.'

'That's the one.'

'Ho, hum, what's he doing here, as if I didn't know?'

'He's after Ben,' said Hal. Then, seeing the alarm growing in Ben's eyes, he added, 'or rather, after the Dewstone.'

That didn't make Ben feel any happier. Had he done all this to have someone else after him? 'Are they as bad as the Numens?' he asked.

'Different,' said Hal. 'Just as nasty.'

'Erica's a sort of cousin of ours,' said Gilly.

Ben stared. 'Cousin?'

'It's difficult to explain,' said Hal. 'We don't really understand it ourselves, but she seems to cross from our world to this one all the time.'

'She's bad news,' said Gilly tersely.

'Why do they want the Dewstone?'

'Power,' said Tarquin. He gave a heaving sigh that set all his scales rattling. 'We dragons don't have this obsession with power. It's all very tiresome. Well, I suppose we shall have to do something about it. Which way did they go?'

Gilly pointed down the hillside.

'Careful,' said Hal. 'We don't know what's happened.'

'Can't see anyone,' said the dragon.

'The Dollop's very near,' said Gilly.

'In that clump of trees?' suggested Tarquin.

'How strange,' said Hal, as they moved cautiously into the shadows of the trees. 'It's quite cold here, and it wasn't at all cold when we were up there by the tower.'

'Sun doesn't get through much, I suppose,' said Gilly, her teeth chattering.

'What sun?' said Ben, as he slipped on some icy leaves.

'Jouri!' called Gilly in a loud voice. 'Jouri, are you here?'

No reply.

Hal and Gilly looked at each other, alarm growing.

'Better go back,' said Hal.

'I don't think we can,' said Gilly, alarmed.

The handful of trees into which they had cheerfully dived was no longer a solitary group, but had turned into a huge and icy forest.

Tarquin's scales were all standing on end. 'Dear me,' he said. 'I don't think this is at all a suitable place. We dragons don't like forests.'

'It wasn't a forest when we came into it,' said Ben.

'It is now,' said Tarquin. 'And I fancy there's game in it, and I believe I can hear hounds, and I'm quite sure that we're the prey.'

He gave an almighty roar of fire, which seared the leaves of the trees above him. Then, with a few beats of his wings, he flew up into the momentary gap, and was gone, before the charred branches settled back into the impenetrable cover.

'Tarquin!' cried Gilly.

'Well,' said Hal. 'Some friend.'

'He may be back,' said Ben. 'Dragons don't behave the way you think they're going to.'

'On our own then,' said Gilly.

'Those hounds are getting nearer, by the sound of it,' said Hal, who was listening intently. 'I wonder whose they are?'

'As if you didn't know,' said Gilly. 'Don't you remember last time we were here? When we were in the caves, and Erica came after us?'

'With those terrible Vemorian hunting dogs.'

Hal looked around. 'We'll have to climb.'

'How?'

Hal looked up at the trees looming over them. Tall trunks, unusually tall for oak trees, rose all round them. These trees were unclimbable, with the nearest branches way above their heads.

'Run,' said Hal.

The hounds knew exactly who they were after, and it wasn't Hal and Gilly. The pack swept towards Ben, who ran as he'd never run before.

He had no idea how far he had gone, or where he was going. He just had to get away from those great dogs, mouths hanging open to show their wicked teeth, jaws flecked with foam.

Ben was terrified of dogs. He had been bitten by a neighbour's collie when he was little, and he had avoided dogs ever since. It was his worst fear, to be cornered by a savage dog – and to Ben, all dogs were savage. Exhausted, he stumbled on, his mind so full of fear that he didn't wonder why the dogs didn't pounce on him and tear him to pieces.

He didn't notice that they were driving him, as though he was a lost sheep.

He didn't notice when he came out of the wood and into the open countryside.

He just ran on and on, only sliding into a collapsed heap when he came to a river.

He looked helplessly up and down the bank. The hounds were snapping at his heels and he whirled his arms in a brave attempt to ward them off. Then he saw a boat, drawn up at the water's edge. With a flying leap, he was on it, panting as he loosened the rope attaching it to the shore and pushed it out to the middle of the river.

The hounds ran backwards and forwards along the bank, as Ben lay down on the hard planks at the bottom of the boat, struggling to get his breath back. He didn't at first notice the silent figure who rose at the end of the boat; then he looked up and saw a man dressed in a dark, sinister livery. This man had pulled out a pole and was now propelling the boat through the water at an increasing speed.

'Who are you?' Ben blurted out.

'A boatman,' said the man.

'Can you put me ashore?' asked Ben. 'I'm sorry I jumped on to your boat, but those dogs were chasing me.'

'The boat was waiting for you,' said the man. 'I'm taking you to where you have to go.'

'And where's that?'

'The palace of the First Lord of Vemoria,' came the chilling reply.

'If we stay in this forest, we'll freeze to death,' said Hal, jumping up and down in an effort to keep himself warm.

Their wild attempt to follow Ben and the pack of hounds had kept them warm enough, but they had had to give up the chase, and they now sat disconsolate under yet another vast and ancient oak.

'I suppose they'll have caught him,' said Gilly.

Hal nodded.

'What will they do to him?'

Hal shrugged. 'Take the Dewstone. That's what they want.'

Gilly leant wearily against the trunk.

'Why Ben?' she said. 'Why did this have to happen to him? He's bullied at school, and then he slips through into this world, and there are people after him, here as well. Just the same. It isn't fair.'

'Not the same at all,' said a very welcome voice.

'Jouri!' said Gilly. 'Jouri, where are you?'

'Up here,' said Jouri.

They peered up into the dark branches.

'Eyes,' said Hal.

'The Dollop,' said Gilly happily.

There was a rustle of leaves, some scrabblings, and the Dollop landed with a thump beside them, swiftly followed by Jouri.

'This is a fine to-do,' he said.

Gilly was staring at the Dollop with a puzzled look on her face. 'I didn't know the Dollop was near,' she said. 'I can't see anything in my mind from him.'

'You wouldn't,' said Jouri. 'We've gone across the border into Vemoria. No telepathy or far-seeing here, it isn't safe.'

'So Ben is in Vemoria?' said Hal.

'Oh, certainly.'

'What will they do to him?' cried Gilly.

'Not much they can do physically,' said Jouri. 'They can't touch him while he's got the Dewstone.'

'The hounds, you mean?'

'Not the hounds, not Erica or Uthar, not the

Wardens; none of them. They won't be able to get within an arm's length of him.'

'So he's all right then. They can't harm him?'

Hal was watching Jouri. 'He isn't all right, is he?'

'They can't hurt him, no,' said Jouri. 'But they'll use every method they can to get him to give up the Dewstone.'

'Trickery?'

'That, and any other form of persuasion they can think up.'

'That could be very hard on Ben,' said Gilly.

'It could,' said Jouri. 'But he's not the same boy as he was when he came through. You don't go through what he has and come out the same. Ben may be tougher than the Vemorians have any idea of.'

Gilly sighed. 'I hope you're right.'

'Meanwhile,' said Jouri, 'we need to get out of this forest and find some shelter.'

'Are we going back into the Thirdlands?' asked Hal, thinking of the warmth they had left behind.

'No, we can't,' said Jouri. 'Even if we wanted to. Which we don't, because I think we need to get as near to Ben as we can.'

'How can we find out where he is?'

'No question about that,' said Jouri. 'He'll be a guest of Uthar's. In Galat.'

'Oh, no,' said Gilly, who had grim memories of the capital of Vemoria.

'Is it still full of Watchers?' asked Hal, thinking of the dark figures standing on the numerous pointed bridges which took people on foot over the network of canals which ran through the city.

'And Wardens?' Gilly shivered as she thought about the highly trained and disciplined secret police who kept control of every citizen's comings and goings.

'I'm afraid so,' said Jouri.

'Won't they be on the lookout for us?' said Hal.

'And what about the Dollop?'

'The Dollop will have to stay behind,' said Jouri. The big grey creature flattened his ears, and made growling noises.

'You'll be needed,' said Jouri. 'There's that Vemorian spy still around. Culun. You'll have to keep an eye on him, make sure he doesn't follow us.'

The Dollop made a few sweeps with his tail and gave one large paw a thoughtful lick.

'Off we go, then,' said Jouri. 'Quickly, now, or we'll all be numb with cold.'

Twenty-Six

*E*RICA KNEW A VICTIM WHEN SHE SAW ONE. 'Leave him to me,' she said. 'Little rat, I know just how to get him to hand over the Dewstone.'

Uthar wasn't so sure. 'This boy is the Red One, he must have strength. Inner resources.'

Erica was scornful. 'Inner resources? Him? Look at him, you can tell what he's like. Bottom of the class, hopeless at games, shortsighted ... he won't stand a chance.'

'You can't lay a finger on him,' warned Uthar. 'Not while he's got the Dewstone.'

'Won't need to,' said Erica with certainty. 'He'll have a very low opinion of himself, I can tell you that. So I just need to work on him a bit. Soften him up. He'll hand over the Dewstone, you wait and see.'

Ben lay huddled in the corner of the cell. The plate of food which one of the surly guards had pushed through to him was beside him, untouched.

Uthar had given clear orders on Erica's advice. 'No contact with him at all. Treat him like an animal. Push food into the cell with a pole. Serve it in a bowl, don't give him anything to eat it with. Give him stale water, make it a nasty colour. We need to keep him hungry and thirsty. Tantalize him with the smell of good food.

Send for a baker, set up an oven nearby, bake some bread. Grill some food under his cell window, so that the smell goes in. And don't anybody clear out his slops.'

The guards listened in silence, keeping their thoughts about their unpleasant duties to themselves.

Uthar turned to the biggest of the guards, a great brooding hulk of a man. 'You,' he said. 'Haven't you got a son?'

'Yes,' said the gorilla, surprised at the question.

'Bit of a lad, is he? Runs a gang, keeps the others where he wants them?'

The guard gave a proud and broken-toothed grin. 'Yeah,' he said. 'Got them all frightened of, him he has.'

'Get him,' said Erica at once. 'Him and a friend, someone nasty.'

Uthar approved of Erica's tactics. 'Yes, she's right. Take them to the boy; tell them to get to work on him.'

'Thought no one could touch him.'

'They can't. Verbal abuse, that's what we're after.'

'Right up my boy's street,' said the hulk approvingly.

And it was. Familiar taunts, heard a hundred times in Ben's other life, poured into his ears. He couldn't sleep. Partly because he was cold and hungry and frightened, and partly because it was the guards' job to keep him awake. By watching through the cell door, and banging and shouting when they saw his eyelids drooping. And as he became more and more tired and hungry, the torment became more and more difficult to endure.

And in the evenings, that girl came. Hal and Gilly's cousin. Calm and reasonable, urging him to give up the struggle.

To hand over the Dewstone.

Then he could eat, and sleep, his tormenters would vanish, he would be an honoured citizen ...

But Ben held the Dewstone in his hand and refused to give in. Giving in doesn't work, he told himself through a haze of weariness and despair. They never stop, they never give up. I don't believe what she says. He couldn't think why they didn't attack him physically; he had expected that.

This, he thought, is worse.

'Yes, it'll be bad for him,' said Jouri. 'They're experts.'

Gilly winced.

Hal clenched his fists, hating to be so useless.

It was a slow, hard journey across the hills and into Vemoria. They were heading for Galat, but by land, instead of the quicker way on the canals and rivers which criss-crossed the country.

'Too dangerous,' said Jouri. 'You look conspicuous, in those odd clothes, and everyone will be on the lookout for foreigners.'

So they could only travel by night. In the daytime they hid, and slept. They all knew the risk they were taking, because in Vemoria everyone, citizens and visitors alike, had to be indoors by curfew, and registered for the night.

Jouri hadn't just stolen clothes, either. He stole a sledge, and every dawn, before anybody was up and about, he went on the prowl for food. As they travelled by, good Vemorians wondered why their hens didn't seem to be laying, or how the dog had managed to get into the larder and steal a whole cheese and two loaves of bread.

Their nightly journeys were hard, cold slogs. Jouri kept the pressure on relentlessly. As he pointed out, they didn't know whether Ben could hold out against

Uthar, Erica and their associated thugs. Or, if he could, how long that would last.

'Erica looks a very nasty piece of work to me,' he said grimly, as they made their way at a snail's pace up a steep and icy hill.

Gilly travelled as though in a dream. Hal, glancing at her distant expression, wondered if she would ever be the way she was before they had crossed the Spellbound Gorge.

Jouri, for his part, knew she wouldn't. 'She may have gifts of seeing, even when you go back to your own world.'

If we do, thought Hal. And gifts of seeing, such as Gilly had demonstrated in the Land of the Gods? Not an accomplishment you'd wish on your worst enemy, he thought bitterly, let alone your sister. He kept going himself through sheer determination. And he was spurred on by the thought of what Ben had done, travelling into that utterly unknown region where dragons fly to bring back the Dewstone.

If he can do that, then I can do this, Hal told himself.

It was a clear and starry night, that last night of their journey. Hal was fascinated by the stars, as he had been when he was here before. They were so bright, so thick in the sky.

So alien.

And Ben, shivering and wakeful in his cell, looked out through the bars at the same alien stars, and thought that he had never been so alone. Not on that distant shore, not in the tower, nowhere.

Then a black cloud drew across the stars, blocking out the starlight from his cramped little space. He sighed. The stars did have a beauty to them, and it was better to look at something rather than nothing. He moved restlessly, trying to make himself more comfortable. Then, as he thought he might risk closing his eyes, a voice came floating down from above his head.

'Go to sleep then. If you don't want to be helped, well, it's entirely up to you.'

Ben felt tears trickling down his cheeks. Was he dreaming? Hallucinating? He couldn't bring himself to believe that the dragon had reappeared. Because if it was just a figment of his imagination, that would be hard to bear.

'Figment of your imagination indeed,' said an indignant Tarquin. 'We dragons aren't figments of anything, let me tell you.'

'Tarquin,' said Ben, sitting up. 'They'll hear you.'

'They will not,' said Tarquin with satisfaction. 'I just gave a huff and a puff or two and they've scarpered. They'll be back, but you can deal with them.'

'I can't,' said Ben desolately. 'They just go on and on at me. There's nothing I can do.'

'I can't stand feebleness,' said the dragon tartly. 'Pull yourself together. Think. Have they laid one finger on you?'

Ben shook his head.

'No, of course they haven't. And why not?'

'I don't know.'

'It's because of the Dewstone! It's a stone of power, don't you realize what that means?'

Ben took the stone out of his pocket and looked at it. 'No,' he said simply.

'Oh, really,' said Tarquin, sounding very impatient. 'It's too bad. Use the Dewstone, boy. Use the Dewstone.'

Ben could hear noises in the distance. Shouts, and heavy running feet.

'Best be off,' said Tarquin. 'Now, remember what I said.'

Creak, and he was gone.

Crash and thump and yell, and they were at the door.

Ben looked at the Dewstone lying small and heavy in his hand. He took a deep breath and held it up.

'Back, you dogs,' he yelled at the top of his voice.

The door burst open, and the gorilla hurtled in. 'You little rat,' he snarled.

Ben held up the Dewstone and advanced on the man, who was at least three times his size.

At the sight of the Dewstone the man blinked and dropped the sword which he had been swirling about this head. It fell with a clatter to the floor as he staggered backwards, holding his arm up to shield his eyes.

The crowd of wardens, watchers and guards who were immediately behind him piled into him, toppling over in all directions. Ben, amazed by the effect the stone had had, took a step forward.

The Dewstone had begun to feel hot in his hand, and as he glanced at it, he could see that it was glowing again. It cast a strange blue light across the cell and on to the livid faces of the assembled hoodlums.

They scattered. Ben walked across the cell and through the open door, not looking to either side, but focusing on the stone.

It was done. He was out, walking along the stone passage which led to the walls of the Palace.

Doors were flung open, flares lit, shadowy figures ran in all directions.

Then, out of the chaos and confusion emerged the tall figure of Uthar, with his daughter beside him.

'Stop,' cried Uthar, in a terrible, ringing voice of authority. 'The Dewstone is not yours. You cannot carry it out of this world. Leave it here with me, I command you.'

Ben looked at the stone, raised his eyebrows, winked at it and turned to face his captors.

'No,' he said.

And he turned on his heels and ran.

Twenty-Seven

*T*HE DOLLOP WAS TRACKING CULUN.
Culun had no idea he was being followed. He was an expert and excellent spy, crafty in all the ways of his trade. However, his training and experience had never covered Dollops, and so his task was easy enough.

Besides, when one Dollop was on the trail, so were all his friends and relations, because of their capacity for feline telepathy. So if the Dollop needed to pause for a wash, or to spend a pleasant hour or so fishing, then another Dollop would be watching and following.

Dollops don't think much, but had the Dollop thought about it, he would have expected Culun to be after Hal and Gilly.

No such thing. Culun was lurking around the City of Towers. Without his lord and master now, and keeping his distance from the other Vemorian snouts and snoopers who frequented the Thirdlands.

That was the first odd thing.

The second odd thing was that Culun then left the City of Towers and headed off into the backwoods. And not any old backwoods, no. Culun was heading for the part where the Numens hung out, where they had fled in rage and frustration.

The Dollop crouched in a tree, invisible against the twiggy, branchy centre, eyes unblinking. His mind was still, but waves of vindictiveness, revenge and malice wafted in from the trio in the barn.

Worst of all was the black, pungent smell of the old, Wild Magic.

The Dollop stirred uneasily, wrinkling his big grey whiskers. He didn't like this at all. He slipped down from the tree and swept silently away into the snow, carrying the warning in his head of a stirring which could mean nothing but trouble.

Trouble for the gods and the demigods.

Trouble and danger for all the creatures who lived in the Thirdlands. And trouble for Tuan and the Gonelands and Vemoria as well.

Hal and Gilly and Jouri had to make the last part of their journey by boat. It was impossible to get into Galat any other way; anyone on foot was viewed with the deepest suspicion.

'We'd be hauled in at once for questioning,' said Jouri. 'Wait here, and I'll have a word with some of the boatmen.'

'He's gone to bribe one,' said Hal, sitting down and stretching his legs out. 'I must say, I've done enough walking. My feet are a mass of blisters.'

'Is it safe, though?' said Gilly. 'You can't trust anyone in Vemoria.'

'Have to,' said Hal, yawning.

They were at a quay, keeping a low profile among sacks and bales waiting to be loaded on to the big barges which plied their way up and down the vast Vemorian canal and river system. It was quiet in the chilly sunshine. A rat scuttled out and across into a warehouse, making Gilly jump and look round to make sure it wasn't one of a crowd.

Then, quite suddenly, all hell broke loose. There were

shouts and yells, and the sound of feet running. One of the great black ships bearing the banner of the ruling Twelve of Vemoria shot past, and then another. They could hear dogs barking.

'It's those hounds again,' shrieked Gilly.

They pressed themselves back into the shadows as the grim figure of Uthar came round the corner, followed by Erica. Clearly in a rage, they moved too fast to see Hal and Gilly, but surged past them and on to the further quay, where the biggest and fastest of the Vemorian black ships was moored.

More running feet, as guards and Wardens, Watchers and shopkeepers swept past. There were shouts and cries of command across the water, more bustle, confusion on the canal as the barges desperately tried to get out of the way. And then, suddenly, silence again.

Hal let out the breath he seemed to have been holding for several minutes. Gilly wiped her brow with the back of her hand. Despite the cold, she was sweating as though it was summer.

'What was all that about?' she said.

'Best not to enquire,' said Hal.

'I hope it was nothing to do with Ben.'

More footsteps. Slower, not running this time. And a clackety-clack noise on the stone quayside.

'Shrink time again,' murmured Hal, pulling Gilly back behind some big wooden boxes.

A shadow fell across in front of them. A short shadow.

And then a most peculiar shadow. Plump, with a tail ...

'Ben,' said Gilly, almost sick with relief.

'Hi, Tarquin,' said Hal, just as relieved, but not wanting to show it.

'Were they after you?' Gilly asked Ben.

He nodded. 'I jumped into a boat, and they thought I'd escaped by water. But I went on across more boats to the other side, and got away. Then Tarquin reappeared, and led me here. Where's Jouri?'

'He was just seeing about a boat to take us into the city.'

'Can't wait,' said Tarquin. 'Best be off.'

'Off where?'

'Out of Vemoria,' said Tarquin.

'Oh, no,' said Hal. 'It's a week's journey.'

'Not if I give you a lift,' said Tarquin. 'Of course, if you'd rather walk, it's entirely up to you.'

Hal's eyes gleamed at the thought of flying with a dragon. 'Won't we be too heavy?'

Tarquin gave a fiery puff of disdain. 'Up you get,' he said. 'Ben will show you how.'

'But what about Jouri?' said Gilly.

'I'll get a message to him,' said Tarquin. 'First things first, and that means you three away from here. Hold tight.'

Vemorians didn't believe in dragons, but there were many who looked out of their windows that night and saw the dragon fly past, a great shadow against the starry sky. Children listened to their parents insisting that dragons and magic didn't exist, and took their own thoughts to bed with them.

The Dollop moved like a grey shadow through the mortals' quarter, and slipped across the boundary into the demigods' streets. He made his way to Ril's house and padded through the archway.

Ril was lounging with his friend Siert, drinking some pink and foaming mixture from a crystal goblet. He put the cup down in surprise as the Dollop perched on his haunches in front of him, regarding him with wide grey eyes.

'What's this?' said Siert. 'Do you suppose he's looking for a home here?'

Even for a demigod, the wave of cat fury which washed across his mind was strong stuff. 'Okay,' he said hastily. 'Forget I said it.'

The Dollop turned his attention to Ril.

'Rubbish,' he said, as the cat's message clarified in his head. 'Nonsense.'

The Dollop sat.

'It isn't possible,' said Ril.

'What are you talking about?' said Siert, who had been attending to his drink.

'Trouble,' said Ril, sourly. 'Those Otherworlders are at the bottom of, I know it.'

'The boy with the Dewstone?'

'Yes. Only the gods know what he may do with it.'

Siert thought for a moment, and pursed his beautiful lips. 'Shouldn't think even they know, if it comes to that.'

'Probably not,' said Ril with a sigh. He put his fingers in his mouth and gave a piercing whistle. There was a flapping sound, and the raven landed beside the Dollop.

The Dollop hissed, and the raven hopped further off. 'Gone to the Spellbound Gorge,' the raven said. 'With the Dewstone. Going back to where they came from. Good riddance, what a shame, what a shame, what a shame.'

'The Spellbound Gorge?' said Ril, frowning. 'Sure?'

'Caw,' said the raven.

'Come along, then,' said Ril.

If crossing the Spellbound Gorge by the narrow bridge was frightening, flying over it at a hundred feet or so by moonlight was much worse. Gilly shut her eyes, hating the feeling at the pit of her stomach, trying to shut out the voices calling to her to jump.

'Earth demons,' said Tarquin over his shoulder. 'Ignore them, and they'll go away.'

'I wish Jouri was here,' thought Gilly. Hal, taking one look at her green face, wished it as well.

Then, thankfully, Tarquin was soaring down to land, which he did with a hefty thump and a spurt of flames which singed a nearby tree.

Hal, Gilly and Ben slid off the dragon and stood, slightly shaky, on the snow-covered ground.

'Safely out of Vemoria,' said Tarquin as he shook his scales back into place and stamped his big talons into the ground just to get the feel of the place. 'And a good thing too. We dragons don't like Vemoria, and one can quite see why.'

'Now what?' said Hal, looking round.

'Off into the sky for me,' said Tarquin. 'It's nearly dawn.'

'Yes,' said Ben sadly. 'You have to go and fly.'

'You'll be gone before long,' said Tarquin, coiling and uncoiling his tail. His scales were glowing a golden colour in the first faint light of dawn. 'So I'll say goodbye.'

Ben looked up at him, his eyes shadowed. 'Goodbye?' He gave a sniff. It was unimaginable to think that, for the first time in his life, he had found a friend and that he was losing him. 'Will I ever see you again?'

'Good heavens, yes. We dragons can go more or less where we want. I'll come and visit you. But you'll be back, you know. I feel it in my scales. Now, I must be off.'

'What do we do?' said Gilly, alarmed to see their ally flex his wings, ready to depart.

'It's entirely up to you,' said the dragon, and with a whoosh of flames and smoke, and a few mighty beats of his wings he was gone.

Ben forlornly watched the spiky, flying silhouette vanish into the distant pale light of morning. 'Goodbye,' he said, waving the Dewstone backwards and forwards in farewell. 'And thank you.'

'Don't do that,' said an imperious voice just behind them.

'It's the head,' said Gilly, taking a step back in surprise.

Ril reached out an arm and grabbed her. 'That was you nearly into the gorge,' he said. 'And don't keep on calling me the head. It makes me feel most uncomfortable.'

'Show respect, yes, respect for an Immortal,' squawked the raven.

'I suppose it was too much to hope that we'd seen the last of you,' said Hal.

'Quiet, Earthscum,' said the raven.

'About the Dewstone,' said Ril, addressing Ben, and watching the stone warily with his glowing green eyes. 'What are you going to do with it?'

'I don't know,' said Ben.

'It gives you power.'

'Which means that everyone will be after me,' said Ben.

'You could be right,' agreed Ril.

'I could give it to someone,' suggested Ben.

'You could, but it might cause a lot of problems.'

'What happened all the time it was with the dragons?'

'Nothing much. Nobody bothered about it, except to have a search for it, now and again.'

'Can't it go back there?'

Ril shook his coppery locks. 'No. The dragon was a guardian, and his time of guardianship has finished.

'Oh.'

'Can it go back with him?' asked Hal. 'To our world?'

'It can go wherever Ben wants it to go.'

'What would happen to it in our world? And to Ben?'

Ril gave a dramatic shudder. 'I don't care even to think about it,' he said.

'I don't want it,' said Ben in a small voice. 'It's beautiful, and I love it, and I'd like to keep it always, but that's no good.' He looked down at the glowing Dewstone and then out across the gorge. 'What would happen if I threw it into the Spellbound Gorge? Does anyone ever go down there?'

'No,' said Ril. 'The gorge is deeper than anyone has ever been, and guarded by strong magic.'

'So the stone would stay there for ever.'

Ril hesitated, and another voice answered for him.

'Few things are for ever, Ben. You are the Red One, who came to find the Dewstone, and you alone could conjure the Dewstone from there. There may come a time when you need the Dewstone again, for reasons which concern you and your family, and also the people in Tuan and Vemoria. If you leave it in the gorge, then until you come again, the Dewstone is safe.'

They had all whirled round as the man spoke.

'The Forester,' said Gilly.

'Have you come to show us the way back?' asked Hal, direct as usual.

'Yes. Ben?'

Ben looked at the Dewstone for the last time. He hesitated, hating to lose it, a moment, raised his arm and tossed it far out into the gorge.

They could see where it fell by the trail of blue light streaming out behind it, sparkling against the rocky sides of the gorge Then the whole gorge and the countryside around was illuminated for a few unforgettable seconds by a great glow of blue and gold.

The Dewstone had gone.

'Come,' said the Forester.

'Goodbye,' said Ril. 'Remember me.'

'What a stupid thing to say,' said Hal, as he went after the others. Were you likely to forget someone who was more than eight foot tall, with a mane of red hair, strange green eyes, and whose head you'd cut off.

'You'd be surprised,' said the Forester. 'Many people from your world forget everything about this one.'

'I shan't,' said Ben, in a whisper.

The Forester looked gravely down at him. 'No, Ben,' he said. 'You'll never forget your time here. You've held the Dewstone, and given it up. Some trace of its magic and power will always stay with you, and it will be waiting for you.'

'Will it?' said Ben, not believing a word of it.

'Look at your hand,' said the Forester.

'It's glowing,' said Gilly.

'No one in your world will be able to see it. Only you and Hal and Gilly because you've travelled into this world.'

'I wish I could stay,' said Ben, thinking of the November gloom which was waiting for him.

'Things will have changed, you'll find,' said the Forester.

'Do we have to cross the gorge?' asked Gilly. 'Because I can't.'

'You can, you know,' said the Forester. 'You've done it once, and if need be, you'll do it again. But it isn't necessary. Look.'

He pointed to a wall which they hadn't noticed

before. It had an arched gateway in it, and from the arch came a tumble of white mist.

'Off you go,' said the Forester. 'Goodbye.'

Epilogue

'WHERE ARE WE?' SAID BEN.
'In our garden,' said Gilly. 'Watch out, the stones on the path are a bit slippery.'

Light from the kitchen window streamed out on to the path. Hal peered into the familiar kitchen. 'No one there,' he said. He opened the back door as quietly as he could, and the three of them slid into the house. Gilly shut the door behind them and turned the key in the lock.

Hal went into the hall. 'Mum?' he called out. 'It's all right. We found Ben.'

Mum appeared, slightly dishevelled as she often was when she was working, and stared at them. 'Was he lost?' she asked, surprised.

'In the fog,' said Gilly.

'Fog? What fog.'

'It doesn't matter,' said Ben quickly.

'Are Erica and her father still here?' said Gilly, lowering her voice.

'Erica? Her father? Gilly, what are you talking about. Are you feeling ill?'

'No, it's just ... Sorry, Mum, I was thinking about something else.'

'I'll be going home now,' said Ben, sidling towards the door.

'You go with him, Hal,' said Mum.

'No, I'll be okay,' said Ben.

'There are some of those boys from your year hanging about.'

'That's all right,' said Ben with quiet confidence. 'I'm not bothered about them.'

'You've grown, Ben,' said Mum, looking at him more closely. 'Shooting up, all of a sudden.'

'Yes, well,' said Ben.

'Are you sure your aunt feeds you properly?' asked Mum. 'I worry about it sometimes. I don't like to interfere, but I sometimes think you'd be better off with your mum.'

'I would,' said Ben with a confidence which made Gilly and Hal exchange looks. 'I'm going to arrange it. Thank you, Mrs Severn. Bye, Hal; bye, Gilly. See you around.'

'Bye Ben.'

'Where are you two going?' said Mum absently, her mind already back on her work.

'Oh, just to look at something in the garden,' said Hal.

'Don't get too cold.'

'Why do you want to come out here again?' asked Gilly. 'It's freezing, and I keep on imagining there's fog rolling up again.'

'We've got to dig up that apple tree,' said Hal. 'We can't leave it there.'

'I'll get a fork,' said Gilly.

'And a saw, to hack the branches off,' said Hal.

'What's that?' asked Mum.

'It's a log,' said Hal. 'From the garden. If we leave it under the stairs it can dry out next to the boiler. For Christmas.'

'What a good idea,' said Mum. 'What is it, apple? Magical.'

'Magical? Why did you say magical?'

'Did I? It just popped into my head. The flames are so pretty when apple burns. Makes you imagine all sorts of things. You look tired, both of you. Has it been a hard day?'

'You could say that,' said Gilly.